GW01066165

Shadow Wolf

Moon Marked, Volume 2

Aimee Easterling

Published by Wetknee Books, 2018.

SHADOW WOLF

First edition. October 8, 2018.

ISBN: 978-1724125798

Written by Aimee Easterling.

Chapter 1

Dried blood coated my cuticles and I blinked, unable to make sense of the unexpected sight. Safely sheltered by werewolves, I'd gone on frequent fur-form expeditions in recent weeks. So maybe that explained the dark circles beneath my fingernails...but since when did I pounce upon unwary rabbits and rip open their throats while I was sleeping?

Seeking clues, I tipped my head upwards to take in the crescent moon then stamped bare feet against bent and splintered grass blades. The strands caught against my toes, clinging as if coated with glue...or with some other halfway-dried and considerably less savory substance.

Blood?

I leapt sideways, the harsh tang of copper following me away from the trampled circle of earth. From the amount of bodily fluids I'd brought along with me, I could only assume I'd waded through the same carcass that had sullied the grass and soil...or had been the one to spill those bodily fluids myself.

There has to be a rational explanation for all of this. Closing my gaping mouth and forcing air to flow more naturally through flaring nostrils, I peered out at the darkened landscape in which I found myself. I was perched atop a rounded knoll, encircled on four sides by tree silhouettes while the moon shone down through a gap in the canopy to illuminate the spot where I now stood...

...Where I stood beside a cloaked figure all too familiar despite the three months since I'd seen him or her last. The being had bought Mama's star ball and absconded with it last spring despite all of my efforts to reclaim the magic....

So I *was* dreaming. I exhaled in relief, pinching my forearm. Unfortunately, the sharp burst of pain failed to wake me back up.

Well, if I had to repeat a three-month-old battle against the owner of my mother's star ball, perhaps this time I'd win the fight. Change the rules, change the game....

To that end, I yanked at the source of my magic, the glow of a sword arcing through the air between me and my enemy. And in instant response, lightning bugs rose in a wave of green-hued reaction, their sheer numbers proving that this was not memory but rather dream. I'd never known so many of the bioluminescent fliers to exist in one location...had rarely even seen a smattering of their neon lights at the wooded edge of the city park where I sometimes went to be alone.

But I wasn't located in my home city any longer. Instead, forest stretched out around me, lacking streetlights, porch lights, even the barest hint of asphalt and diesel fumes to pinpoint a nearby a road.

Where was I? And why had I moved this frequently remembered battle from the abandoned theater in which it had actually occurred to an idyllic spot lifted from a fairy tale?

All of these thoughts flooded my neurons in the time it took for the lightning bugs to wink out and return the scene to near darkness. Meanwhile, as if my enemy had been waiting for the return of my attention, cloaked arms rose in a flicker of black on black. Then a shining orb levitated out of the being's right sleeve.

Now I could see my opponent easily as he—she?—beckoned me forward with one curving finger. *Come*, the gesture demanded as Mama's star ball winked at me from around the being's gloved hand. I cocked my head in response to the magic's odd behavior. Then the glowing star ball shifted, stretched...and turned into a whip that lashed out faster than a cobra to encircle my arms and chest.

The magic *burned*. Cut through my silk kimono and almost—but not quite—prevented me from noticing how dramatically this nightmare had gone off the rails of its usual script.

Since when was there a lasso involved in our battle? Since when did I wear kimonos? Since when did the anonymous being I fought against wield magic I had yet to understand?

"Who are you?" I demanded, not even trying to bring up my magical sword to sever the imprisoning connection that pulled me one step closer to my nemesis, then another. Because I could feel my mother's essence within the glowing rope restraining me—who knew what would happen if I cut that soulbound magic in half to free myself?

The words had been a parry, meant only to win me another moment in which to think. But, to my surprise, my opponent didn't ignore them. Instead, lasso pressure on my stomach eased as a hooded head cocked to one side in mimicry of my own earlier gesture. I could almost smell the being's confusion as he or she paused rather than continuing to reel me in.

Scent. Yes, of course I should use every weapon at my disposal if this really was a face-to-face meeting with my nemesis rather than a rehashed memory-turned-nightmare.

But the breeze was flowing from behind me, the air too dry to be redolent with identifying scents. And as the wind whipped unbound hair against my cheekbones, I flinched, realizing what I should have gathered from the start.

The body I inhabited wasn't my own—how could I have missed that? Instead, I stood in the skin of my dead mother. More slender than my real body, a trifle shorter, and enfolded in the subtle haze of jasmine that always preceded my mother whenever she entered a room.

Then my lips opened and Mama's voice spoke through me. "Master..." she started, chilling me to my core. So the cloaked being had figured out how to use Mama's star ball since I'd last been in his or her presence. Had figured out how to use her magic...and her as well.

But before Mama could bow to the Master further, before I could beg forgiveness for letting her fall into such a trap, my earlier wish was granted. I slipped out of my mother's body and woke in my own bed with a start.

Chapter 2

It was half past four in the morning, but I couldn't close my eyes, let alone return to slumber. Not even after examining now-clean fingers and toes to reassure myself that the strange confrontation had only been a figment of my dreaming mind's imagination.

Instead, I lay between soft sheets, listening to the silence of Gunner's mansion. During the day, the halls filled with chatter and laughter. But in the wee hours of night, the place became positively peaceful with everyone sleeping.

Well, everyone except for me.

It wasn't the first time I'd risen before dawn, unable to accept a wolf pack's confining safety. So I pushed out of bed, pulled on clothes, and headed downstairs to the empty courtyard. There I drew upon my star ball and dueling against nobody, stretching muscles well toned from previously insomniacal bouts.

Fighting, at least, tired me enough so the questions and worries circling through my mind lowered their volume. Was I doing the right thing choosing momentary safety for Kira while going against every instinct toward self preservation that our parents had taught? *Slash, lunge.* Would I come to regret accepting a so-called "job" that involved doing whatever I wanted while being paid more than I'd previously made as a teacher and cage-fighter combined? *Riposte, retreat.*

There were no more answers this morning than there had been last Tuesday or two weeks ago Wednesday or any other time I'd come out here to fight shadows rather than snuggle up in my bed like a good little wolf. Still, I couldn't help smiling despite the sweat burning my eyeballs when the inevitable morning bickering rose with the sun, proving that my sister was now wide awake and much perkier than she'd been the day before.

"So you think it's *funny* to let me fall into the toilet first thing in the morning?" Kira snarked from the east end of the first floor—the massive kitchen where everyone except me tended to congregate as soon as they got up.

"Come on, pipsqueak. Today's the big day. Give me a break."

Looked like my kid sister was back on task as self-appointed toilet monitor. And one of our house mates—Tank this time—had relieved himself in the night without remembering to re-lower that all-important white seat.

Kira grows more wolf-like and less fox-like every day, I noted, not sure how I felt about the matter. Foxes were reserved and elusive. But wolves, I'd found, expressed their affections best in the physical realm.

Sure enough, the crack of a snapping towel evoked a squeak from my sister even as another house mate, Crow this time, stated the obvious: "That's *our* bathroom, puppy. You and Mai have your own on the third floor. So if you fell in, it's your own da...ahem...*darn* fault."

Logic, apparently, had no impact upon my sister. "I live in this entire *house*, not locked in the attic like a crazy auntie. For example, I spend a lot of time in the kitchen *cooking*. So if you want any of my bacon, you'll start putting down the toilet seat *everywhere*."

"Ooh, *burn*," Allen murmured, far too quietly for the neighbors to hear him. My fox senses, on the other hand, caught the comment quite ably...along with a salty sweet scent that had me slowing my morning exercise into a cool down. Perhaps being part of a wolf pack wasn't so terrible if it came with bacon at the exact moment my stomach started growling....

Except even as I started imagining breakfast, the hairs on the back of my neck prickled. My nostrils flared, my muscles tightened. There was something nearing, something watching....

Bacon abruptly forgotten, I whirled in reaction, raising my sword as I turned to face the stalking wolf.

OR, RATHER, TO FACE the two-legged wolf in human clothing. Gunner raised one eyebrow at the pointy blade just barely indenting the skin beneath his Adam's apple. Then, ignoring my weapon, he held out a mug of chamomile tea, the sweetness of honey curling off the surface as the leader of the wolf pack I lived amidst greeted me aloud.

"Tough night?"

I shook my head, not so much in denial as in a refusal to rehash my dream landscape verbally. And in response, Gunner's open face shuttered ever so slightly as if he was more disappointed by my evasion than at being greeted by the sharp tip of a sword.

But just as quickly, Gunner regained his customary smile, jiggling the mug between us so the ceramic clanked against my magically-created weapon. "We should do something fun before Kira's custody hearing," the ever-patient werewolf suggested. "Go for a run somewhere wild before we're due in court. Or...shopping? Does Kira like shopping?"

"My sister loves nothing better then spending other people's money," I admitted, allowing my sword to diffuse back into a magical blob that slid along my skin to form a bracelet, a belt, a sheathed knife at my left ankle. In front of me, Gunner didn't even twitch at this evidence of my kitsune nature. "But we shouldn't spoil her," I added. "And, anyway, I've got other plans."

"Plans?"

This time I accepted the mug my companion brandished in my direction, pretending that I needed to all of my attention to prevent a spill. Taking a sip, I noted that Gunner had steeped the tea just the way I liked it, not so long it turned bitter but not so short that it was simply sweetened water with a hint of aroma to turn hot liquid into soothing tea water.

The flavor was perfect...but my gut clenched anyway. Because it was time for our inevitable weekly ritual. No one managed to slip away from the pack without extensive explanation, but I couldn't afford to let any of the werewolves I lived with know where I went on Tuesday afternoons. In lieu of the truth, I always ended up stuttering through an entirely unbelievable explanation, and the wolves around me always smiled grimly and allowed me to lie.

Fox, not wolf, I reminded myself. The important matter here wasn't these shifters' identity. It was reaching my destination without catching their eye.

Luckily, the street was crowded and I found it easy to slide in behind a group of laughing ladies, pressing forward until I was just barely inside their personal space. The quartet was too animated to notice the intrusion as they recounted some past adventure involving beaches and dancing and far too many margaritas...all while striding toward the foot of the bridge I very much needed to find a way across.

"...and then Doug took off his shirt! Bared everything! Potbelly and all!" one woman crowed, and I threw my head back and laughed right alongside them...the gesture doubling as a show of solidarity and an easy way to hide my face from sight.

Unfortunately, the ladies didn't cross the bridge I wanted to go over, and there was no way I could veer away from the group without being noticed at this point. So I flowed down the block along with the chattering humans. Slipped through the doorway of a high-end boutique when the women whooshed inside in a close-knit cluster. Then, glancing back over one shoulder and noting the werewolves' lack of attention, I yanked the door back open and sprinted toward the river behind the nearby row of shops.

"Hey!" The shout was redolent with alpha compulsion, but it didn't faze me. Not when the command was aimed at werewolves and even more at those who belonged to a pack.

Instead, I was a fox. So the order rolled over me like water off a duck's back.

"Stop!" the wolf continued. But his word didn't even slow my footsteps. Instead, I leapt onto the horizontal limb of a

sycamore, raced across smooth bark until I was directly above deep water, then I dove directly in.

I REMEMBERED ONE MILLISECOND before breaching the surface that I couldn't soak my current outfit. Not when I'd donned my best clothes for Kira's custody hearing and lacked the time to drop by a laundromat and bake the pant suit dry on my way back.

Good thing I'd spent the last few weeks learning to better manage my magic.

Yanking at my star ball with a facility I hadn't possessed three months earlier, I was encased in a skin of water-repellant magic by the time I slid beneath the river's murky surface. And while a more experienced kitsune might have been able to sequester an air pocket for ease of breathing, I was content to simply block out encroaching liquid as I allowed the river to carry me slowly downstream.

I *did* produce a cone-shaped protrusion around each ear, though. And I was gratified to find that the spur-of-the-moment hearing aids were quite efficient at picking up sound emanating from the nearby shoreline.

"The boss didn't send us here to track down strays," one voice growled. "If the bastard wants to swim the river, he'll be a Claremont problem on the other side."

Smiling as the river flowed around me, I couldn't help but agree. Another benefit of being a fox around werewolves—the latter were so rigid in their pack structure that it was remarkably easy to wriggle my way beneath the rules.

For example, meeting my mentor outside Atwood territory and without Gunner's permission meant Ransom wouldn't be able to argue his brother had broken his promise. The convoluted reasoning was immensely satisfying...but the second shifter's words wiped all amusement off my lips.

"That wasn't a 'he', you idiot. It was a female." This voice sounded vaguely familiar, as if the second watcher might have been one of the shifters who'd turned the tide at the showdown in the theater three months earlier. And his scent? Had there been more to it than the mantle of Atwood ozone rising through the stench of city garbage?

I racked my brain but came up with nothing else by way of memory. I could only hope that meant my own flavor had been similarly muted by distance, and just as generically werewolf-like as I'd been led to believe.

With an effort, I turned my body around to push back upstream against the current. Wolves might not be curious, but foxes were. And I had a feeling the duo might let drop identifying information if I hovered here long enough.

"If it's a female," the first male started....

But now my lungs were burning, the opposite shore seeming an impossible distance away from where I hovered. If I popped back up in the river so close to where I'd gone under, this pair of werewolves might risk the gray area of the boundary and come in after me.

So, reluctantly, I relinquished my spot in the river. Changed my ear cones into flippers. And pushed toward my original destination with all my strength.

Whoever these shifters answered to, they weren't my problem. Not when I was, and always would be, a lone fox rather than a wolf.

Chapter 4

I emerged, gasping, beneath the overhang of a bushy outcrop on the Claremont side of the watercourse. The watchers had lost interest, I noticed, retreating back to their bridge-side vantage point. Relieved that their tenacity was so subpar, I rose out of the water, pushed through the brush to the open area further from the river...then felt myself spinning sideways as hands grabbed and tugged on my left arm.

Shifter. My sense of smell was still catching up to my reeling balance, but I could tell I was being manhandled by a werewolf due to the superhuman speed my attacker possessed. Too bad my diffusely dispersed star ball meant a sword refused to materialize in a timely manner....

I couldn't afford to shift into fox form, either. Not when kitsunes were verboten everywhere other than in Gunner's mansion.

That didn't make me entirely helpless, however.

Instead, I let momentum carry me groundward, curling in upon myself as I fell so I hit the leaf litter already spinning into a somersault. With any luck, my opponent would still be shuffling backwards into two-footed stability after such an all-out attack, a lapse I planned to take full advantage of by ramming into his knees....

Or, rather, into *her* knees. I identified my teacher's signature scent of spring rain, roses, and ozone even as I bowled her over, was apologizing profusely before she thudded butt-first atop the hard ground.

"Elle, I'm so sorry. Did I hurt you?"

My roll had carried me past my opponent and back to my feet, so it was an easy matter to reach down in preparation for pulling the slender brunette erect beside me. And as I did so, I felt my forehead furrow in confusion. Why was my teacher—Crow's mate, a resident of Ransom's pack—waiting for me here rather than half a mile down river where we usually met each other? Had Crow received a message that he failed to deliver? Had our illicit meetings finally been found out?

"You were late," my mentor answered the question I should have asked rather than the one I'd actually managed even as her hand clamping down on mine. "I was worried."

Not so worried that her lupine nature didn't show through, however. One moment she was my smart, protective teacher. The next, her eyes glistened with amusement and I braced myself against the inevitable yank intended to tumble me onto the ground.

Strangely, though, Elle merely scratched my palm rather than pulling me downward. A tiny trickle of blood welled up even as she retreated, her expression more fox-like than wolf-like as she licked her fingernail clean.

"What?" I started as icy cold ran up my arm and across my shoulder. My mentor's eyes glowed red, my stomach lurched in answer...

...Then I was bending over backwards, twisting my body into a series of contortions that might have amused an audi-

Swiveling in my seat, I sighed at the abrupt appearance of Simon's gloomy visage. The lanky human must have slipped in even later than I had, and unfortunately his professional opinion as a social worker was likely to hold more weight than a grand gesture on Gunner's part. Especially with a judge who was now *smiling* despite the entirely out-of-line discussion taking place in his court of law.

"Because...?" the judge prodded.

"The point being—as always in these cases—the well-being of the child." Simon glanced in my direction briefly, his grimace suggesting that he hadn't forgotten the glimpse of paranormal happenings he'd been privy to three months earlier. The social worker had seen just enough to fuel wild guesses...but I could tell the conclusions he'd come to made him even less impressed by the idea of me raising an innocent child than he had been before.

Luckily, Simon wasn't our social worker any longer. Because the move to Gunner's mansion had changed the district overseeing our case...a point which Stephanie was quick to point out. "I'm the one making a recommendation on behalf of the state," the middle-aged woman said loudly, half-rising as she turned her attention back and forth between Simon and the judge.

I held my breath, half expecting her to make another dig about a teenage girl living among so many unattached and unrelated male personages. But Gunner had worked his magic on Stephanie over the last few months just as thoroughly he had tamed everyone else in his vicinity. There had been cookouts, thoughtful questions about her family, and in the end the alpha had ingratiated himself so thoroughly that the social worker had started inviting *us* into *her* home.

So I shouldn't have been surprised when Stephanie barked back at Simon without hesitation, her tone as fierce as that of any territorial wolf. "I am entirely in favor of this adoption being carried out as requested. The Fairchild family deserves to remain intact."

"Hmm," the judge answered, not even glancing at Stephanie as he jerked his chin toward Simon, giving the latter an opening in which to elaborate.

And Simon didn't fail him either. "After watching Kira live on pasta and peanut butter, start fights with little or no provocation, and get kicked out of two schools over the past six months," Simon intoned gloomily, "I strongly believe the opposite. Kira would be better off living in a halfway house rather than remaining under her sister's inappropriate care."

Chapter 6

Reprieve came from an unexpected the direction. The judge, who I'd thought was looking for the slimmest excuse to wrest Kira out of my custody, banged his gavel before Stephanie could do more than open her mouth for what was bound to be a heated rebuttal.

"As much as I'm enjoying this farce, I have a dinner date," the man said dryly. "So we'll conclude this case on Friday. If anyone has additional evidence they hope to discuss at that time, I recommend you file it *in advance*."

Then we were rising, watching the judge sweep out the back door while Simon stormed out the front. It wasn't a success, but at least we'd been granted a stay of execution. And after thanking Stephanie for her support, the fun-loving werewolves around me immediately leapt onto the idea of a celebratory hunt.

"Wildacres?" Allen suggested, naming the former retreat center that had become the pack's customary hunting grounds in the months since Kira and I been folded into their pack-in-exile. Because the loss of Mama's star ball meant Kira wouldn't be able to shift until she materialized magic of her own making. Good thing Gunner just so happened to have purchased a two-hundred-acre retreat complex, complete with trails wide enough for a teen-driven golf cart to speed along beside wolves and one lone kitsune.

I glanced at my sister, expecting her to take the choice of venue as her due. But Kira wasn't even following the conversation, I realized. Instead, her legs wobbled and her lips quivered, giving me just enough warning to encircle her waist with one supportive arm before she sagged.

"Kira?" I asked, trying to remember if I'd fed her lunch. No, I hadn't. But my sister had been in the middle of the pack at the noon hour—surely the guys had stuffed her to the gills.

"I'm *fine*." Now Kira sounded like herself...and looked like herself as she batted away my supporting arm too. "And you guys don't have to go to Wildacres just for me either. I'd rather read in the car than hang out with you losers anyway."

Now every eye was focused on my sister, four sets of werewolf eyebrows lowering in synchronicity that owed much more to their attachment to Kira than it did to the bonds of pack. "Losers, huh?" Tank countered while I was still trying to decide if the legal setback was really what had shaken up my sister so thoroughly or whether her health had faded so much so quickly. "You can't even beat us with an engine under your a...butt. You want to beg off because you're *afraid*."

For all of his wolfishness, Tank was surprisingly subtle when he wanted to be. Okay, so maybe "subtle" wasn't quite the right word for it. But, whatever the proper adjective, Tank's jibe effectively staved off Kira's emotional retreat and tempted her to engage with her usual flourish.

"Am not!" the child countered.

"Are too!" came the lawyer's skillful repartee.

As our other companions cheerfully joined into the bickering, we all ambled together out to Gunner's SUV then rode through rush hour traffic to Wildacres. And if an odd hole opened up in my stomach as I watched my sister's easy camaraderie with the werewolves, it was worth it for the smile that ended up on her formerly grumpy face.

WE STRIPPED AND SHIFTED outside the abandoned retreat center's main building, in a parking lot surrounded by trees that reminded me for one split second of the setting of my nightmare. Perhaps that's why I hesitated before transforming, stood for ten long seconds absolutely naked but with my panties still dangling from lax fingertips.

"Mai?" Gunner's warm presence pulled me out of my brown study, his eyes searing into my own. Unlike me, he and the guys were accustomed to shifting in company. In fact, the other three werewolves were already in lupine form, frolicking beside my sister who had thoroughly regained her usual good humor during the preceding ride.

"Sorry." I shook my head and dropped the scrap of fabric onto the pile of clothing between us, trying to keep my gaze as carefully face-oriented as Gunner's was. I was a fox, though, not a werewolf. So perhaps it was merely vulpine curiosity that made my eyes drift south....

Whatever the reason, I couldn't stop myself from assessing the alpha's corded muscles and sun-warmed angles. My gaze stroked skin that I would have liked to follow with my hands....

Well, that's not happening. Covering up my illicit daydream, I acted as I should have minutes earlier. I closed my eyes for one split second, then I exploded into the form of my fox.

Fur itched as it pushed out of a human body. Fingernails yanked themselves forward into claw points. My tail grew lightning quickly into a fifth appendage, its fluffy bulk providing an acrobatic grace I could never muster on two legs.

And as I gave in to the fox's body, the preceding awkwardness faded in the face of the challenge of a slanted tree trunk. Rough bark on paw pads. The scrabble of claws against wood as I almost slipped but didn't fall.

Then I was laughing down at my companion from five feet above him...just as the low whir of the golf cart's electric engine started the race.

Immediately, every head turned toward Kira's conveyance. This was why we came here. To hunt sometimes, but more often just to run. And with Kira zipping down the path already, every wolf was hard-wired to give chase.

Foxes, on the other hand, have more choice in the matter. Yes, I craved a triumph...but I was more flexible about how I achieved that goal. Cutting down into a ravine then back up the other side might have been cheating by werewolf standards, but how can you cheat when there are no rules?

Wind, fur, mud, rush. This was the best part of denning with werewolves—the opportunity and ability to race.

Which is how I came to be diving out of the woods to rejoin the others as Kira sped toward the finish line. Behind her, a line of panting werewolves jockeyed for position, Gunner in the lead as his claws tore up the soft earth.

Only nobody in our pack triumphed. Instead, the golf cart skidded sideways as it stopped prematurely, the wolves between me and Kira growling as they picked up on clues I was unable to see or smell from my spot on the other side of the ditch.

Then a tall figure rose up beside my sister's shoulder. A grimly smiling werewolf, but not a stranger unfortunately.

"Well met, brother," offered the pack leader who had sent Gunner into exile. Then his hand came down upon Kira's unprotected neck.

Chapter 7

Mud squished between my toes and my sword tingled to life in abruptly human hands as I lunged toward the male threatening my sister. I half expected Gunner to get there first, frowned as I saw him instead shift and sink into the mud with human shoulders bent earthward. "Pack leader," my former protector murmured. "I have done everything you requested. I ask that you do the same."

The brothers' compromise. Of course. Ransom had ignored the fact that I was a kitsune three months earlier in exchange for Gunner's fealty. Now it appeared that the time had come for the latter to pay up.

A rock dug into my left instep as I swerved sideways to steer clear of the alpha I'd thought was on my side but who might actually be forced to do Ransom's bidding. No matter. I could trust Kira to roll sideways at the proper moment. So all I had to do was...

...twist away from the five wolves who had slid out of the trees and into my sight line while my attention was riveted upon Gunner and his brother. The newcomers reeked of Atwood ozone, their trajectory clearly intended to cut me off from their leader's unprotected backside. And, based on the way they lunged forward without even glancing toward Ransom for permission, I had to guess they'd also caught a glimpse of my illicit fox-related shifting....

Suddenly, I couldn't spare a thought for Kira's predicament or for Gunner's precarious loyalty. Instead, it was all I could do to push off the mud-slick pathway and slip between two teeth-bared muzzles as sharp fangs grazed the skin of my unclad thigh.

Now they growled, the sounds smug with imminent triumph. No wonder when I was entirely surrounded, five wolves spreading in a tight circle that pushed me toward a laughing enemy each time I backed away from one of his pack mates. My sword could only do so much in tight quarters and I was surprised the quintet hadn't already leapt forward and taken me down into the muck.

Their strange reluctance to finish what they'd started, however, couldn't last forever. So I hacked desperately, the flurry of blows insufficient to break me free of the circle but enough to send my enemies back a single step.

A whimper. The scent of Kira's terror. I couldn't spare a glance in her direction, but she was clearly in distress now.

So I tried something I'd been pondering ever since Elle bested me with a scratch from her finger. I flicked my sword back instead of forward, seared a larger cut than I'd intended onto my left forearm.

My own blood tasted nothing like a rabbit's. Instead, it was sweet and at the same time peppery, full of magic I'd yet to learn how to tap.

Necessity is the mother of invention, I decided, closing my eyes for one split second and pulling every burst of power down my spine and into my feet.

Mud splattered around me, slipping through my parted lips and onto my tongue. The soil was gritty and vile, tasting strangely of iron even though the scarlet seeping from my leg and arm shouldn't have made it all the way to the ground so quickly.

Unfortunately, a mouthful of mud was all I got out of the endeavor. No shards of star ball pushed my enemies backwards. No wall of magic prevented their approach. Instead, the wolves pressed in closer, the fear in their eyes promising danger.

Because frightened wolves tend to react predictably. They squash their terror, then they attack.

"DON'T TOUCH ME!"

Kira's voice rang out as I tried—and failed—to rebuild my sword from a lax and diffuse star ball. Her silence up until this point had been carefully calculated, I knew, to prevent distraction. The fact she was now speaking, her voice more shriek than words, proved that the situation was growing worse outside my circle of werewolves even as I edged closer and closer to losing the current fight.

Desperation hadn't been enough to turn the tables in my favor, but worry over my sister pushed me forward where the impulse for self-preservation had been insufficient. Giving up on rematerializing a physical weapon, I instead slid into my fox skin as easily as a swimmer dives beneath the water. And, like a swimmer, I immediately felt gravity recede beneath my feet.

Human, I'd been unable to escape the ring of werewolves. Vulpine, I leapt over the closest wolf's head and landed atop his well-padded rump light as an errant sunbeam.

Unfortunately, my opponent wasn't a fan of sunbeams on his butt. He whirled, teeth snapping shut a millimeter from my fox tail...or perhaps he *did* end up with a mouthful of white-tipped hairs after all. The small loss of bodily matter was irrelevant, however, when I was already ten feet distant, scampering toward a sister who I now saw was engaged in a struggle of her own with two familiar-scented Atwood males.

Ah, the bridge watchers had made a reappearance. So Ransom had kept an eye on us after all. Hadn't been as hands-off about Gunner's exile as he'd initially appeared.

And as if my puzzle-piecing had caught the pack leader's attention, Ransom's eyes abruptly bored into me from only a few feet distant. Meanwhile, Tank, Allen, and Crow were all belly down in the mud in wolf form, resolutely peering the other way as one of the bridge watchers wrenched Kira's right arm up behind her back.

They aren't going to help her. This sign of cowardice on the part of my supposed allies hit me strangely, deep and low like a punch in the gut. For the last three months, every one of our house mates had treated Kira like a beloved kid sister. But now, when push came to shove, they were just going to let her be manhandled without batting a lash?

Well, *I* wasn't so fickle with my loyalties. I bared my teeth, unsure what a single fox could do against masses of wolves but ready to make a stab at some sort of offensive anyway.

Only, before I could act, Ransom growled out an order. "Rein in your woman," he demanded, gaze turning now to his kneeling, naked sibling.

And Gunner didn't even attempt to disobey his brother. Didn't jerk his chin and give his men the right to help us out of our predicament.

Instead, he lifted his head from perusing the mud. Met my eyes. Used my debt against me.

"Mai, stop," Gunner said curtly. And, predictably, the kitsune necessity to repay all of the kindness Gunner had showed me and Kira froze my body mid-swivel. Wrenched me back to humanity. Knocked me into the mud so hard that I didn't get back up.

Chapter 8

D espite dark glares from my former enemies, the wolves I landed amidst didn't tear into me. Instead, they glanced once at Gunner, his verbal claim sufficient to mark me as ineligible for use as lunch meat. Then they shifted in tandem, revealing long scratches up their backs and shoulders that looked far more like the effects of human nails than like any wound I might have inflicted during the battle that came before.

I didn't have long to puzzle over that inconsistency however. Because the werewolves I'd spent the last three months sharing a house with had risen to human feet at the same moment, stepping forward to take up where Ransom's underlings had left off. Allen, Crow, and Tank had always treated me and Kira with gentlemanly deference back at the Atwood mansion. Now, though, the first two grabbed hold of my arms while Tank took custody of my sister on the far side of the racetrack-turned-battlefield.

"I have your word," Gunner growled between us, his back still bent in deference to his brother even though I could taste the former's frustration permeating the air. "The sisters are mine to manage. As ordered, I kept them far away from your pack."

Rather than replying, Ransom gazed at my unclad breasts in a very unshifter-like show of lasciviousness. Not that he seemed particularly interested in me as a sex object or even as a potential enemy. Instead, I got the distinct impression he was staring in an effort to draw his brother's attention to himself.

Gunner, however, kept his gaze carefully trained on the mud. So Ransom was forced to move on to words.

"Are you still sniffing after unwilling tail, brother?" the pack leader asked after one long moment during which my skin prickled with the intensity of his perusal. "If she hasn't put out by now, she's just using you for your money. You're no Casanova, but surely even you know that."

Gunner raised his head in response and I winced, surprised to find that this jab at the younger brother's manhood—or perhaps at my honor—had succeeded where Ransom's earlier efforts at breaking through his brother's illusory show of submission had resoundingly failed. The already loaded air vibrated with electricity now as the younger brother leveraged himself upright, the mud caking his legs from knees to ankles doing nothing to diminish the power of his broad-shouldered stance.

Gunner was magnificent, I noted. A pack leader in bearing if not by birth order. In contrast, Ransom looked like an upstart, no less dangerous but lacking the restraint and maturity his younger brother had in spades.

No wonder Ransom flared his nostrils and continued with his verbal parries. "I've invited two dozen pack princesses to this year's gathering," he said, smirking so broadly his final word was distorted. "They've all accepted, of course, because I'm the world's most eligible bachelor. I plan to try them on for size this week, in ones and twos and threes if you know what I mean." He wiggled dark eyebrows before finishing. "I'm sure a

few of the discards will give you the time of day, though, brother. It's painfully obvious you can't get laid on your own."

And that was *almost* the last straw. Around us, werewolf
shoulders bent down beneath the force of Gunner's displeasure, the concept of Ransom running through virginal inno-
cents like kleenexes hitting the alpha where it hurt. Any second
now, Gunner's already stretched nerves would snap and he'd
say something that neither he nor his brother were capable of
forgetting.

Which was a shame since I was beginning to understand
the point of the preceding banter. Ransom was attempting, in
the least efficient way possible, to rewind the brothers' relationship into the past.

After all, Gunner and Ransom had been a solid team when
I first met them. The elder brother led the pair on wild goose
chases while the younger brother propped up his sibling at all
costs.

Which made Ransom's choice to assert his independence
three months ago nonsensical. Apparently now the pack leader
had returned to his right mind.

Unfortunately, an alpha werewolf can't just ask for assistance. So I sighed, pulled free of my supposed jailers, then took
one step toward Ransom with diplomatic words waiting on my
lips.

The male I faced, though, was nothing like his brother. He
didn't raise brows in question and treat me like an equal when
I inserted myself into a conversation that didn't apply to me.

Instead, the pack leader's eyes skimmed over my mud-cov-
ered body, a smirk rising onto his lips. "Can't resist a real man,
can you, baby?"

Baby, really? And, to my eternal regret, the words I pushed into the ensuing silence came out cockeyed, less like a fox's smooth sidestep and more like a sally led by a werewolf's bared teeth. "My favors aren't for sale," I started. "But you think your brother's are, don't you? What do you need Gunner to do for you now?"

Five minutes ago, I'd thought the situation had already hit rock bottom. But, yep, I'd managed to make it significantly worse. Because Gunner's arm twitched as if he wanted to press between me and his brother...or possibly to wring my ornery neck.

For his part, Ransom *did* turn his attention away from needling Gunner. But as the pack leader's shoulders expanded with alpha aggression, I felt far less capable than Gunner had been of standing up beneath his brother's discontent.

Only...the pack leader didn't eviscerate me, either verbally or otherwise. Instead, his eyes slid sideways to land on the male guarding my back. "Actually, Crow, I came to talk about my cousin. Since when do you let Elle cross into Claremont territory and train kitsunes on the sly?"

Chapter 9

The mention of kitsunes startled a growl from my former assailants, but none of the five moved to act on their ire. So I took a deep breath and accepted that it was time to live up to the promise I'd made Elle when we first started getting together just beyond the edge of Atwood land.

"Are you going to get into trouble for meeting me here?" I'd asked tentatively the first time we'd slipped our minders and visited Claremont territory on the down low. I didn't want to lose my teacher before lessons even started...but I also didn't want to be responsible for a werewolf getting tossed out of her pack if she wanted to stay.

"I'm Ransom's favorite cousin. He wouldn't do anything to me," Elle had promised with a soothing smile. *"But Gunner and Crow aren't currently in his good graces. We have to play this carefully to protect the guys."*

So we'd met in secret, Elle passing along coded messages through her mate that Crow pretended not to understand the meaning of. For my part, I'd evaded Gunner's questions with far less agility, but the plausible deniability was still very much there.

And now the time had finally come to deny the males' involvement. After everything Elle had done for me, I refused to let my mentor down.

"Crow had no idea what was happening," I proclaimed, striding past far too many narrow-eyed shifters as I forced myself to approach the angry Atwood pack leader one step at a time. "No one here knew where I was going. The fault was entirely mine."

"Mai..." Kira started, her voice suddenly young and scared as the reality of our predicament broke through her youthful belief that no harm could come to those she cared about. I hated to worry her, but I trusted Gunner to protect my sister. And I didn't want Ransom's attention focused on Kira for any longer than it already had.

So I pulled out a metaphorical red cape and waved it in front of the bull—or is that bully? "If you want to punish someone for training me," I continued, standing tall at my full five foot zero inches, "surely you're not afraid to tackle a kitsune on your own."

THE WORDS WERE PURE bravado, and I braced myself to be punished by the pack leader now that he had an actual offense to lay at my doorstep. But I'd underestimated Gunner's protective instincts. Because his proximity warmed my backside mere seconds before his hands gently moved me out of his path.

Then the two brothers were facing each other directly, only a few inches of air standing between shoulders that were equally broad and features so similar they were almost twin-like. "An alpha knows what happens in his territory," Gunner growled, completely ruining my efforts to keep him out of harm's way.

"It was my choice to allow Mai and Elle to spend time together. I wanted my kitsune to be properly trained."

I half expected Ransom to laugh at both of us. After all, Gunner and I were naked, muddy, and sorely outnumbered. But, instead, the Atwood pack leader puffed himself up further as if facing a rival, his muscles tensing as he attempted—and failed—to stare his brother down.

"*Your* territory?" Ransom muttered finally. Even I could tell that the words had been ill-chosen on Gunner's part. Because the younger brother was still on Atwood land despite having been exiled from clan central. And no pack leader likes having his property impinged upon in front of his men.

"*My* corner of *your* territory," Gunner corrected himself. He cleared his throat, remembered at last to avert his eyes from the supposedly un-meetable gaze of his older sibling. "I've finished clearing the city of malcontents as ordered, pack leader. Are you ready to put me to use so I can quit twiddling my thumbs?"

There. *That* was the answer Ransom had come here to draw out of his sibling. Gunner's head bowed in submission, and the tension between the pack leader and his brother dissipated like fog beneath summer sun.

Still, Ransom waited a moment before accepting his brother's rewording. But then he clapped his sibling on the back...just a little too hard.

"Oh, are you ready to end your vacation, brother? Ready to help me manage our entire territory...and reap the sweet rewards?"

The reminder of the waiting pack princesses made something dark flare within Gunner's eyes for one split second. But his words were pure docility.

"Of course, pack leader," Gunner answered, speaking to the mud rather than to his brother's face. "I come whenever you care to call."

Chapter 10

"Wildacres is safer than the city," Gunner whispered rapidly once we'd all donned clothes and had begun our preparations to depart. The alpha had drawn me aside at the edge of the trees where we could keep an eye on Kira without being in the thick of the action. And while his need to bid me farewell was heartening, any potential coziness was diminished by the fact that two other shifters currently hung on their alpha's every word.

"I can have the electricity on within the hour," Allen noted, tapping at his smart phone's screen, his eyes carefully steering clear of mine.

"Can't do much about the state of the buildings but food delivery is easily achievable," Crow agreed. "Clothing too. And the water comes from a well, so that should work right now."

It was as if I'd become a problem to be managed rather than an honorary pack mate. Which, combined with the way Gunner continued to stare me down like an alpha dominating a recalcitrant underling, made me tempted to rewrite my understanding of our shared past.

After all, Gunner told his brother he'd merely been "twiddling his thumbs" during the preceding season. Which begged the question—had he really become attached to me and Kira, or was his assistance nothing more than the actions of a bored alpha latching onto the nearest available task?

"Stay put," Gunner commanded now, gaze flicking over my shoulder for one split second while he continued barking orders. "Don't give Ransom any reason to go back on his word. Keep your sister close to you."

Well, if Gunner could stick to business then I could also. The trouble was—having Gunner leave us didn't only tug at my heart strings, it also threatened the safe future I thought we'd built for Kira during the preceding months. After all, without Gunner protecting us in person, what was to prevent other werewolves from poaching on his claim? How were we going to win the judge and social worker over to our point of view?

"I *promise* no harm will come to you within my territory," Gunner said, as if he was able to read the doubt in my posture. "I..." he continued. Then, shaking his head, he turned his attention to his hovering lackeys. "Give us a minute."

They didn't flee as quickly as Ransom's underlings would have. Instead, for the first time since the Atwood pack leader had shown up where he wasn't invited, a hint of amusement filtered into Allen's eyes. Meanwhile, Crow coughed into his hand as if smothering amusement, and I had to restrain an urge to kick both bozos in the knees.

Was our separation just a big joke to them? Had our inclusion in their pack for three full months meant nothing that it could be so easily set aside now?

Then—"Look at me," Gunner demanded, drawing my attention away from his receding pack mates. But rather than continuing to relay orders, he reached out slow as molasses. Let fingers trace my cheekbones as he cupped my face in both of his hands.

He's just a touchy-feely werewolf trying to keep me focused, I told myself. But it was hard to believe the lie when my companion leaned in close enough so his breath hovered above my lips like skittish butterflies.

For half a second, I inhaled Gunner's exhale. Smelled his rich, warm aroma. Felt his proximity heating my skin.

Then his mouth landed, hard as a sword thrust.

If our first kiss had been a subtle feint on my part, our second kiss was a ploy of ownership on his. Later, I would realize that every shifter present watched the claiming. Later, I would realize that Gunner was backing up his earlier words with a show of possession that no werewolf could fail to comprehend.

At the time, though, the kiss came and went so quickly I was left reeling and unsure of gravity. And by the time I'd regained my balance, Gunner was already twenty feet distant, his long, lean back the only part of his body visible to my searching eyes.

"Don't let your sister do anything stupid," he told Kira in passing. Then, without a single farewell glance in my direction, he gathered up his pack mates, rejoined his brother, and disappeared into one of the waiting minivans.

TOGETHER, KIRA AND I watched the last taillight recede from the parking area. Darkness was descending rapidly, the sprawling complex that had once housed a busy retreat center looming above us rather than inviting us inside.

"We're staying here?" my sister asked, her voice higher-pitched than usual. She sounded younger now than when wolves had first come into our lives three months earlier. As if becoming part of a pack then losing that protection had lowered her toughness quotient by 100%.

Or maybe it was my sister's unexplained weakness that sagged her shoulders and slowed her footsteps. Whatever the problem, it wasn't going to be solved by waiting here for an absent alpha to remember we continued to exist.

So—"No," I answered, letting my hand linger on the teen's shoulder for one long moment as I pondered next steps forward. I wasn't sure exactly how I was going to manage it, but I intended to find the source of Kira's malaise and solve it, even if—as I suspected—the effort involved hunting down the cloaked figure who had bought and absconded with Mama's star ball.

Which might take a while, given the fact that neither Gunner nor I had found any trace of our enemy's trail in the three months since we'd last seen the being. I'd cross that bridge when I came to it, however. First, I pulled out my cell phone to call the sole person who might miss us if we didn't make it home in the next few days.

While waiting for Kira's social worker to answer, I circled the SUV Gunner and his pack mates had left behind them. It was a nice gesture on their part...or so I thought until I realized the vehicle was locked up tight.

"...then leave a message after the beep," Stephanie's voice mail told me even as Kira offered up a suggestion on the vehicle front.

"We could hot-wire it," my kid sister noted, her eyes trained on her own cell phone, which currently played a video her social worker would very much *not* approve of. "But we'd have to break a window to get at the steering column and we'd need a screwdriver and some other tools...."

I shushed her rapidly as a strident beep promised Stephanie's phone was now recording every word we uttered. "Hey, this is Mai Fairchild," I answered on autopilot while mulling over my sister's suggestion. We *might* be able to break into the vehicle and hot-wire it, but we'd stand out like a sore thumb driving down the interstate with splintered glass in place of a window pane.

Not that I knew where we were going. But I trusted that once we had wheels under us, the path forward would become more clear.

"Kira and I decided to go camping for a couple of days," I continued, patting at my pockets in hopes a multi-tool would suddenly materialize. No such luck. Which left the golf cart as our more realistic option. Too bad the battery-operated vehicle would likely traverse no more than twenty miles before stranding us in an even less habitable spot.

So...maybe we should trust Gunner and stay here after all. His underlings were nothing if not efficient, which meant we'd soon possess both electricity and food. If Kira and I had actually been camping, we would have enjoyed far fewer amenities. Too bad the hairs on the back of my neck begged me to get the hell out of there...and fast.

"Mai," Kira started, all but tugging on my sleeve as she attempted to grab my attention. Once again I shushed her, rattled off farewells to her social worker's answering machine before ending the call.

Only when I removed the phone from my ear did I realize why my sister's eyes had widened in horror. She wasn't nudging me onward out of ordinary teen impatience. Instead, she was alerting me to the fact that we weren't alone after all.

No, there were wolves howling in the distance. And, by the sound of it, they were heading our way.

Chapter 11

"Take the battery out of your phone," I said evenly while matching actions to words with my own device. I couldn't be sure that these shifters had used technology to track us, but I certainly didn't intend to leave that particular barn door wide open for the next time....

Unfortunately, my fingernail caught and bent on the hard plastic in the process, and I swore using language I'd been trying to eradicate from my vocabulary while putting on a good face for Stephanie and her ilk. Not that invective was going to harm Kira more than the wolves now close enough so scents of fur and electricity pressed hard against my nose linings. Brushing aside my brain's wild attempts to think of anything other than the upcoming battle, I fumbled at the key of the only mode of transportation we had at our disposal—the slow and not-so-steady golf cart.

Only that *wasn't* our only mode of transportation, as I realized when Kira's battery slid into her pocket and landed with a soft metallic *clink*. "What?" I started. But my sister was way ahead of me, digging into the denim at her hip with slender fingers then hoisting a key fob erect.

"Tank must have put it there," she crowed, her words tumbling over themselves even as we changed trajectories, running now toward the opposite side of the lot. "I've been teaching him magic tricks, but I didn't realize he'd gotten so *good* at it. Way to go, Tank!"

For the first time in over an hour, Kira's eyes sparkled, reflecting my own rekindling hope. Because if we could outrun the wolves and flee the property that was beginning to feel like a death trap, perhaps we'd survive this ambush after all....

Then we were piling inside the vehicle Gunner had left behind him, slamming the doors, and twisting the engine into roaring life. Back wheels spun on gravel as I pushed the SUV into a three-point turn far faster than was advisable....

Not quite fast enough, though, since eyes were materializing behind us, pupils glowing yellow against the descending dark.

There were at least a dozen werewolves loping out of the forest now. From inside the vehicle, I couldn't smell whether they were Atwood shifters or strangers. All I knew was that they were hungry and *huge*.

Which meant we should be burning rubber in our haste to escape them. Only...my foot slipped sideways rather than punching into the gas pedal. And Gunner's order—*"Stay put"*—rang through my head like a tolling bell.

My debt, it appeared, was working against me. Rather than rushing to evade our attackers, I only managed to clench white-knuckled fingers around the steering wheel as the vehicle beneath me rolled to a gravel-crunching halt.

I wasn't alone, however. Instead—"Gunner always said you were an idiot!" Kira roared, the second-hand insult strangely effective at loosening my debt's hold. Meanwhile, my sister's hands pushed down on my knee even as my muscles reasserted themselves. Then we were speeding out of the parking lot, racing away from wolves howling angrily in our wake.

"He said that?" I asked the back of Kira's head as she turned to raise her middle finger and stick out her tongue at our rapidly receding pursuers. I would have worried that she'd make them even hungrier for our blood...but we had a vehicle and they didn't, so the point was now moot.

"Naw," Kira answered, turning back to face forward. She was panting and sweaty, I noted. Nothing like the teenager who could have run twice that distance without batting a lash. "But I thought a bit of anger might get you moving," she continued, proving that even if her body was oddly weak nothing had happened to her quick mind.

Then, changing gears in an instant, my sister bombarded me with questions of her own. "Where are we going?" she demanded. "Shouldn't we call Gunner to pick us up?"

And I *wanted* to drop the mess into an alpha's lap, I really did. I craved a life so simple I could depend upon werewolves to enfold us into their pack and bail us out of all predicaments.

But Gunner's bond to his brother had proven more resilient than any ties he'd built to us over a single season. And whatever was wrong with Kira seemed to be getting worse and worse.

So I shook my head, stilled Kira's fingers when she went to replace the battery in her cell phone. "No, we'll just drive for a while," I decided. Drive...and see if my instinctive fox nature could come up with a solution to Kira's malaise that my rational side hadn't discovered quite yet.

Loosening my stranglehold on the steering wheel, I let my fox have her head.

Chapter 12

A while turned into five long hours, the beginning of which was just high-speed meandering, attempting not to drive around in circles while ensuring the wolves at Wildacres had lost our trail. But then Kira conked out beside me and I had time to fully consider the impossibility of the task I'd set for myself.

I needed to figure out the source of and solution to the illness that had beset my sister. To track down the owner of my mother's star ball and vanquish the being who had won out over me three months earlier. Those mysteries had seemed unsolvable with Gunner's vast resources at my disposal. What chance did I have of finding the answers on my own now?

While thinking, I raised my left forearm to my mouth, sucking at the wound I'd self-inflicted in an attempt to escape from Ransom's lackeys earlier. The sore was no longer bleeding, but fox nature prompted me to purify the gash with the healing power of good, clean saliva. The task wasn't very palatable from a human perspective, but at least it soothed my nerves.

Soothed my nerves...and reminded me of how awful I probably looked. Glancing at myself in the rear-view mirror, I had to laugh at the mud and gunk splattering my clothes and skin from head to foot. One dirty wound down, ten thousand cuts and scratches still to go.

I wasn't about to lick my entire body, which meant most me of me would remain filthy. But at least I could drive without smearing the steering wheel with drying blood....

To that end, I switched to my sword hand to clean the red speckles off my thumb and forefinger. Only this blood wasn't of my own making. Instead, the particles bit into my tongue, sharp as pepper...then filled me with an epiphany-laden euphoria that came and went in the time it took to release a single breath.

This was the magic Elle had tapped into. This was the boost I needed to figure out where the solution to my dilemmas lay.

This was also likely highly dangerous. Why else would my mentor have warned about the ability of a werewolf to use kitsune blood without mentioning the reverse possibility?

Still.... Beside me, Kira curled in on herself as if shielding an aching belly. Outside, strangers rolled past in their cars. There was no one left but me to protect my sister. So, before I could rethink the avenue of exploration, I sucked up the last of the wolf blood on my finger....

"Take me to the solution to Kira's problem," I said aloud even as my head threatened to float out of the vehicle like a helium balloon. In response, the power channeled inward, hardened, pointed...pulled the steering wheel toward the north.

I FOLLOWED THE VAGUE hints of directions for the rest of afternoon and evening, until our SUV crunched to a halt in a tree-lined dead end. Kira was still soundly sleeping, and her fetal-position body looked so childlike that I hated to wake her up. Still, the niggle of intuition in my stomach urged me onward, so I shook Kira's shoulder gently then a little harder yet.

"Is it morning?" my sister murmured, voice hoarse and raspy. Back when Kira enjoyed access to our mother's star ball, she used to leap from bed to mischief in less time than it took for me to open my eyes and wipe away the sleepy dust. Now, though, my sister was groggy and grumpy, barely willing to follow me out of the SUV and into the night.

"I miss my star ball," the teenager complained as we picked our way across the roadbed and into the richly scented woodland beyond it. As if proving her point, a low-hanging limb smacked into her face, evoking a string of those exact same words my sister wasn't supposed to know the meaning of.

I started to laugh at her drama-queen impersonation—after all, moonlight illuminated the forest quite sufficiently for fox-assisted eyes. But there was actual blood on my sister's cheekbone, suggesting this was more than an act intended to send us back to the SUV to sleep.

No, my sister really was floundering without Mama's star ball, humanity reasserting itself as the borrowed magic faded away. Luckily, I could see well enough for the both of us. Readjusting our positions, I tucked Kira's fingers into one of my belt loops then began holding each limb carefully sideways until we were both long past.

We continued that way for perhaps three quarters of a mile, the traveling made easier once we latched onto a game trail that had been beaten into the earth. Here and there, I caught faint hints of canine. But the scents were old and might have been made by farm dogs rather than by wolves...or so I let myself believe.

Finally, the ground rose beneath our feet, giving us the option of turning sideways as the deer had done or smashing our own path through blackberry thickets up to the crest. My fox instinct whispered *upward*, and my human nature agreed that the rise would be an easily defensible location just in case the afore-mentioned scents belonged to shifters rather than to pets.

"Just a little further," I promised, easing Kira through the tangle. She whimpered as thorns snagged in her hair and tore at her cheekbones, but the girl didn't complain as I less than agilely untangled strand after strand.

A Kira too tired to even protest being manhandled was a sad sight indeed, and in desperation I turned to stories to keep her there with me. "Did I ever tell you what it was like when I got my star ball?" I asked, feeling her head shake slightly from side to side as I picked a thorny twig out of her hair.

Taking that motion as an indication of moderate interest, I dove straight into an anecdote from my past. "It appeared above my pillow the morning I turned thirteen," I offered, gently pressing Kira back onto the path as the thorn let loose its hold on her head. "You've gotta remember, I wasn't lucky enough to have a borrowed star ball from the time I was a toddler the way you did. So this was the first time I'd been able to change into fox form."

My sister murmured understanding, which was enough to keep me leading her on up hill while telling a story I'd never relayed to anyone previously. "It was scary and exciting to be an animal," I told her. "And, I'm ashamed to say, I ended up barfing all over my birthday cake...."

The tiniest trickle of a giggle was the nicest sound I'd heard all day. Then we were out of the briers, sinking down to sit side by side on a soft bed of tall grasses.

"But my birthday was *two months ago*," Kira rebutted after a moment, the impatience in her voice making her sound almost like her old self again. "And I *don't* have a star ball. I *can't* shift."

"So maybe biology doesn't always operate by the calendar," I answered. Then, ignoring the twinge of conscience in my stomach, I voiced a vow I had no way to keep. "Your magic will show up soon, I promise. And, if not, I'll find a way to get Mama's star ball back."

Chapter 13

I fell asleep begging my mother for answers, and maybe that explained my dream. A dream of fingers raking across rippling muscles, a male convulsing above and within me as I shivered in triumph and disgust.

Disgust because I was prostituting my body. And triumph because I'd harvested enough blood this time to sedate my Master...and also to empower myself.

"Stay," the male murmured as I disentangled myself from his body. "You're a wildcat. I dig it. There's more where that came from."

"Another night," I purred, licking scarlet liquid from beneath my fingernails and watching as the werewolf beside me slipped down into unbreachable slumber. Like the others, he'd remember nothing more than sharp-edged pleasure the following morning. Once again, the harvest had been a success.

I might as well have been alone now as the moon shone in through a screened tent window, the male's slumber a reprieve from possession and pretend. But the Master wouldn't like it if I lingered here indefinitely. So I licked more blood from around my cuticles, daintily spitting the liquid into a tiny bottle provided for this exact purpose before moving on to the next.

Without my star ball, I couldn't outright disobey direct orders...but my jailer didn't know enough to hedge every potential gap in the defensive wall that hemmed me in. So after cleaning my right hand and moving on to my left index finger, this time I swallowed instead of spitting.

And, immediately, the body I was inhabiting melded deeper around me. The world, which had been muffled and distant, roared closer in a haze of cricket song and hazy moonlight. Werewolf energy blossomed beneath my skin, and for one short moment my abilities amped up so far I was able to not only grasp blindly for my daughter but also to speak.

"If you can hear me, Mai, know this is your heritage," I murmured, feeling blindly through the void that separated us. "Your soul in someone else's body. It takes werewolf blood, but it is possible to achieve...."

I wanted to show her, to turn my head toward a mirror and let the red of possessed eyes shine out of someone else's features. After all, Mai likely couldn't hear me, but maybe she could see the potential if I tried....

Unfortunately, there were no mirrors present, and the closest body of water was too far for me to reach before the Master's will tugged me back onto the accepted path. Already, I could feel this dozenth try at communication failing. Could feel a tug in my belly drawing me away from the tent, across closely shorn grass, to the drop-off point at the edge of the field.

I tucked the bottle of liquid behind a rock in the designated area, pain coursing through me as I tried once again to disobey. Because I knew the Master's use of this magic would be worse than the possession that had harvested it. I knew...

...nothing as my conscious began to fade. The body I was inhabiting shuddered as my soul wisped into static. But I clung on with incorporeal fingers, unwilling to disappear before righting my own wrong.

Because I'd wrenched my star ball from my body to protect my daughters. How bold I'd been to think I might change the course of history when the trail into the future branched and branched and branched again.

And yet...I continued to be bold. Because every peek I mustered past the veil of the present promised dangers to my offspring. And I refused to leave them walking blindly into the mists.

So I used the last drop of werewolf blood still embedded in my palm to power one final attempt. "Be careful," I tried...and failed...to warn them.

Then, once again, I lost myself into the dark.

I WOKE WITH COPPER on my tongue and the vile memory of my mother—myself?—having sex with a stranger. My shoulders hunched in horror as I spat red-tinged liquid out onto the grass.

"Mai?" Kira murmured beside me. She woke slowly, the same dawn light that had broken me out of the nightmare prompting her to unfold, stretch, leverage her slender torso semi-upright.

She looked terrible this morning. Her lips were gray around the edges. Her eyes were barely slitted open. Her voice sounded like a fox's moan of discontent.

And there was nothing I could do about it except mimic werewolves. So I slipped my hand onto her shoulder for a quick dose of comfort then pulled her upright to follow the path my gut suggested downhill through the trees. *The Master is this way*, a voice in my head seemed to murmur, its tone midway between Mama's and my own.

But as much as I wanted to find our enemy and settle this issue once and for all, we had to pass through the forest to get to that point. And my life in a concrete jungle had left me with few wildcrafting skills to call upon. Perhaps that's why it took pretty much the entire day to pick our way through a forest that seemed to fold in on itself and grow larger by the hour, every passing moment making me doubt my instincts more and more.

"I'm thirsty," Kira whined as hot afternoon sunlight turned the forest into a sauna. Then she brightened, pointed—"Look! There's a stream..."

"...Which you're not drinking out of." I grabbed the teen's arm and pulled her away from the enticing rivulet of water. Wildcrafting wasn't my strong suit, but even I knew that imbibing untreated water in a forest full of deer poop was a recipe for disaster. This trek would be significantly less pleasant if we both came down with the runs.

Of course, I could have shifted into fox form and drunk from the creek without repercussions, but that would have been akin to smacking my kid sister in the face with her loss. Instead, I swallowed against the scratchiness in my throat, turned resolutely away from the water, then beat a path straight up a forty-five degree hillside in the direction my gut told me led toward the solution for my sister's malaise.

We walked forever, until my head pounded from the heat, drowning out cicadas, my thoughts, and even Kira's dismal panting in my wake. "I really think if we'd stayed in that valley, that creek would have led us right here eventually," my companion groused after we'd crested a rise, gone down the other side, and ended up beside a creek eerily similar to the one we'd started out beside.

I opened my mouth to agree, then hesitated as strongly scented air flowed across my palate and down into my throat. The breeze was sharp with ozone, and now that our feet weren't shuffling through leaf litter I was positive I heard something unusual rising over the insects' relentless song.

Yep, there it was again—a yelp piercing the thrum of the cicadas, a growl so deep it vibrated against my very bones.

Kira's dark eyes met mine, hers wide with worry. So she'd heard the same thing I had. Had heard, and was reacting in the way any smart fox would when facing predators larger than themselves—with the urge to flee.

But Kira looked like death warmed over and the tug in my gut told me the solution lay before us rather than behind. So, taking my sister's hand, I tugged her around a curve in the hillside...and straight into an amphitheater full of wolves.

Chapter 14

The indentation in the earth was massive, big enough to seat perhaps a thousand audience members upon the grassy steps that led from where we were standing down toward a similarly open and grass-lined stage. Which meant the two hundred or so shifters lounging both two-legged and four-legged before us should have been a measly showing barely sufficient to tempt the entertainment—two battling were-wolves—out of bed.

But the air was electric with excitement. The fighters moved so quickly I couldn't tell one from the other. And every audience member leaned forward with such intensity that none noticed when Kira and I stepped out through the trees behind their backs.

Which was a good thing since it gave me time to scan the audience, seeking the solution to Kira's increasing weakness. The answer must be here somewhere—surely it wasn't coincidence that we'd come all this way and ended up right back within the ozone-scented Atwood pack....

There, my instincts whispered, the tug in my gut pulling me one step further out into the open before fading away entirely. Whatever was aiming me had turned my chin a little left of center, and I saw at once what I'd been guided toward.

Ransom lounged upon a gilded throne at the edge of the stage area, one leg flung up over the armrest and an empty goblet dangling laxly from the opposite hand. A male whispered in his left ear while a simpering female topped up whatever he was drinking. And as the battling wolves before him tumbled and growled with such ferocity that even my bloodthirsty sister winced in sympathy, Ransom just smiled wider and lifted his goblet back to his lips.

"When we were kids, Ransom was the rash one," Gunner had told me many months earlier. *"He made...mistakes...and was glad to have me as his compass."*

Now, as a chill ran up my spine, I suddenly regretted never digging into what those mistakes consisted of. Why hadn't I found time to ask the reason the younger brother acted in many ways like the older son?

Because Gunner was unshakably loyal to his brother, that's why. Because I trusted the alpha who had protected Kira so selflessly. Trusted him...and didn't want to see him hurt.

There in the amphitheater, Ransom's eyes met mine with gleeful malice. And I accepted at last that I might have let the younger sibling's trust cloud the instinctive judgment of my fox.

Because the brows of the Atwood pack leader lifted sardonically, then his eyes flitted sideways to take in Kira sagging beside me. The gesture was a clear warning, and I wished by all that was holy that I'd thought to stash my sister in the forest before walking boldly into the evening entertainment of the Atwood pack.

Hoping to correct my mistake, I scanned the crowd in search of familiar faces. Tank, Allen, Crow, and Elle were present, I noted thankfully. All four were clustered on a back step, close enough so Kira could likely reach them before Ransom's men had time to attack.

But I made no move to push her toward them, not wanting to relinquish my sister to second-tier protectors no matter how loyal they might be. Instead, I scanned the crowd again, hoping Gunner would materialize and use his strength to ensure Kira remained entirely safe.

If the alpha was present, though, his large form was lost amid the watching shifters. And now the wolf battle amped up to the point where it drew even Ransom's jaded eye...and my own skittish attention.

There was fur in the air as the combatants rolled together across the stage area. The growls turned so fierce that I wanted to spray them with a water hose, and the front row of the audience scuttled backwards as the fighters impinged upon their personal space. I couldn't understand why any pack leader in his right mind would allow such a battle to continue unhindered...

...and as if sensing my concern the pair froze, one wolf clamped down upon the other's jugular. So this was it. The bloody end that a suddenly silent audience had been anticipating.

"Mai, that's..." Kira whispered. But I already knew what she was trying to point out. After all, I'd been smelling Gunner for several long minutes—the only surprise was that he was the losing wolf on the bottom rather than the triumphant wolf on top.

Then the tables turned...or rather the wolves.

The pause, it turned out, had been a gathering of energy rather than incipient submission. Because without regard to his enemy's knife-sharp canines, Gunner shifted as he lunged upward. Muscled arms twisted, one behind his back and the other out in front. He heaved the black wolf through the air to thud so hard against Ransom's throne that the latter lay still where he'd fallen. Then straightening, Gunner stood tall and naked, appearing more like a pack leader than his brother did upon his throne.

The crowd erupted into an exuberant roar of shouts and clapping, but Gunner didn't even acknowledge the noisy jubilation. Instead, his gaze me mine, the touch hard hard like the kiss we'd shared back at Wildacres...then soft like a hand on my back guiding me through an open door.

Warmth, greeting, appreciation...then fear on my behalf. All of that flickered across Gunner's features one second before all expression faded away.

Unfortunately, Ransom was just as sharp as his brother and I doubted he'd missed the preceding exchange. But the pack leader didn't remark upon our wordless greeting, merely clapped slowly and sarcastically as the losing combatant clambered to his feet and slunk, still four-legged, away into the crowd.

"Well done, little brother," Ransom broadcast loudly enough for me to hear from the top step. Clearly, the preceding battle had merely been a game in his estimation, and as he motioned toward the audience I saw for the first time what had been intended as the prize.

Because a woman in a translucent white dress hovered at the edge of the assembled shifters. She was all pack princess—young and beautiful. And, apparently, for sale to the highest bidder now.

"Congratulations," Ransom continued. "You have won a night with the lovely Lucinda by your side."

Chapter 15

I think I must have gasped. Whatever the reason, Kira's right hand clamped down upon my left arm so hard I lost all circulation. And, in reaction, I forced my spine to straighten, my face to remain as serene as Gunner's still was.

But Ransom wasn't done teasing us. "Stay, stay, the show's not over!" he proclaimed, halting shifters who had begun standing and shaking tension out of their bodies in preparation for departure. Obediently, they stilled and sank back down upon the grass even as I pushed Kira toward the promised safety of Tank and his companions.

Because something was about to happen. I felt it, knew Ransom's trouble centered around me rather than around the brother he loved to hate.

And, sure enough, this time Ransom gestured across the audience in my direction. "Tonight will be a double header," he continued. "Who wants to fight for the right to take Mai Fairchild to his bed?"

Two hundred werewolves swiveled and stared at me, their eyes hungry, interested...and not friendly in the least. They were all young, I noticed, nearly all males too. As if the families and oldsters had opted out of Ransom's summer gathering, knowing what sort of craziness was likely to occur therein.

But Gunner rained on their parade quite admirably. Although already half entangled in Lucinda, he still managed to step forward and proclaim "Mai is *mine*" around the female shifter's curly updo.

Everyone else quaked before the younger sibling's growl, but Ransom merely laughed. "Don't get greedy, little brother. You already hold one bitch in heat. What use would you have for a fox?"

And, just like that, the cat came thoroughly out of the bag. *"Kitsune"..."Fox"..."Magic"*—words rose above the crowd in waves of whispers. I caught only hints of the ensuing conversation, but what I heard was pretty much what I'd come expect.

Only their pack leader's presence was preventing the crowd from turning into a mob intent upon tearing me to pieces. So this seemed like the perfect opportunity to raise my voice and announce: "I fight for myself."

Just like that, the few males who had stood when Ransom asked for takers promptly flopped back down onto the ground. "What, nobody?" Ransom laughed even as he raised one eyebrow. "Well, if none of you are brave enough to fight a kitsune, I'm game. No weapons, though. Skin and fur only. I'll beat you fair and square, little vixen. Then you'll scream with pleasure inside my tent."

I GLANCED AT NEITHER Gunner nor Kira, knowing the horror that would be displayed on both of their faces. Because Ransom had placed me in an impossible position. If I won, the pack would assume I'd used kitsune powers and disembowel me...and my sister also. If I lost, I'd be forced to sleep with a male I found distasteful—a matter worsened by my sister's wide eyes and Gunner's apparent inclination to tear his brother apart.

Buying time, I descended slowly, letting my sword dissipate into a ball of glowing magic and noting in the process which nearby werewolves stood their ground and which fell subtly back before my approach. There were more of the latter than the former...but winning still didn't seem like the smartest path to saving Kira's life.

For his part, Ransom was shucking off his clothing as if performing a strip tease, one slow article at a time. His eyes were on his brother instead of me, however. And as Gunner's color rose, I hastened my own steps.

"I'm ready," I told the nearly naked pack leader upon reaching the recessed stage. I hadn't shifted...I didn't particularly want to wave my fox tail in front of a pack of wolves when so severely outnumbered. Instead, I spread my legs and braced myself, lowering my weight a little and preparing for whatever attack Ransom chose to dish out.

I'd braced myself...but I still wasn't ready for the speed of my opponent's charge. One moment the pack leader was stepping out of boxers, the next he was spinning toward me, four-legged and covered in fur. I barely had time to leap out of his path before he barreled into the spot where I'd been standing. Then he twisted sideways and bit at my leg so unexpectedly that I only had one second to ponder whether to cheat and use my star ball for protection or not.

No, I decided. A fox would. A wolf wouldn't. So, instead of materializing the metallic cuff that could have saved my skin quite literally, I leapt upward and kicked out at my opponent's face.

Of course, magic aside, the move was the only one at my disposal. No wonder Ransom was prepared for my evasive jump. His head whipped sideways even as he flung himself airborne after me. And I yelped as sharp teeth bit into the skin of my hip.

Gunner's growl rent the air even as Ransom released me. And I knew without being told that, the next time my enemy's teeth contacted, the younger brother would join the fight.

Which couldn't happen. Not when Gunner was doing everything he could to maintain a relationship with his brother. Not when I was still unsure whether my instinct was right and the male I fought against was the Master and the solution to Kira's malaise.

But I couldn't turn fox or utilize my magic. So what alternative did I really have?

For his part, Ransom was enjoying the hunt. Rather than attacking again directly, he pushed me backwards subtly but unerringly, guiding my footsteps toward the first line of seating in an effort to trip me up.

Despite knowing what was happening, I had no real alternative. So I took another step backward...then something seared across my stomach like a combination of ice and fire. As if the magic guiding me here had rematerialized three times stronger than when it had left me. Only, tiredness now dragged down my body rather than the euphoria of wolf blood buoying me up.

"What?" I murmured, glancing down at my own belly. Ransom was too far away to have done the damage, but whatever had hit me was sharp and effective. Because a thin line of blood now pushed up through my clothing. Meanwhile, behind my back, the audience's reaction was out of proportion to the minor wound.

While my attention had been focused elsewhere, whispers from the crowd had turned into a cacophony. A man grunted, a woman screamed.

Leaping sideways, I bought enough leeway to peer back at the watching shifters. To my surprise, it wasn't the prospect of a kitsune fighting their pack leader that had the werewolves riled up. In fact, they weren't even gazing in our direction at all.

Instead, shifters batted at themselves wildly. First they hit their own arms and legs as if trying to squash a biting insect. Then they pushed against each other, descending into an unruly snarl like dogs with cans tied around their tails.

One male turned to face the forest, revealing a long line of blood dripping through his shirt much like mine was doing. Meanwhile, at the edge of the stage only twenty feet distant, Lucinda leapt out of Gunner's arms and onto the grass.

Or, rather, she appeared to have been *pushed* out, slung sideways by a being we could neither smell nor see. I could sense the spirit, though. Could almost taste its barely contained anger....

So Mama *had* been the one guiding me after all. The unexplainable wound in my belly matched the location of the instinct that had led me to this location in the first place. Had her daughter's blood been sufficient to turn her corporeal? Was that why she was now able to come to my aid?

Whatever the nuts and bolts of the matter, I appreciated Mama's attempt to break up the fighting. It was just too bad she'd chosen to show herself so thoroughly right in front of a pack of angry wolves.

Chapter 16

"Stop!" I yelled, forgetting I was supposed to defend myself from Ransom as I instead dove toward the younger Atwood who appeared to be next in line for my mother's wrath. Because I wasn't so sure Mama understood who was and wasn't her enemy. And I couldn't bear the thought of harm coming to the alpha who had protected me and my sister for so long.

Only...I appeared to be moving in the wrong direction. Because Ransom—now human—roared like a stuck pig, slapping himself in the face as a scratch rose along the side of his jaw. Then another cut opened up the skin half an inch away from his eyeball, which raised the pitch of the shifter's roar into a scream.

"Mai, grab it!" Elle yelled from the top step of the amphitheater. Kira was gone—one glance told me that—hopefully spirited away by one or all of the guys we'd lived with back in the city. But my mentor was trying to push her way toward me...an attempt doomed to failure given the state of the milling crowd.

Her words, however, were enough to provide direction. If Elle thought grabbing my mother would make a difference, then I'd do everything in my power to touch Mama's spirit self.

Unfortunately, the ghost in the amphitheater was still invisible. And her attack upon Ransom was so erratic—hitting his feet, his head, and his buttocks in short order—that I didn't even know where to begin my defense.

Or my human self didn't. Sliding out of my clothes and into my fox skin, however, opened up new avenues to explore. Whiskers twitched with shifting air currents. Superior nostrils caught the faintest hint of my mother's favorite jasmine perfume winding around my nose.

She was hovering in a tornado of fury around the pack leader's head, I gathered. Too high for me to reach even if I regained my human stature.

On the other hand....

Leaping onto Ransom's shoulders was the work of a single second, fox paws spreading to catch my balance even as the werewolf attempted to bat me aside. Mama was close enough now that I could have reached out and touched her. But there was one more thing I needed to do first.

Because blood, I gathered, was the key to kitsune powers. Good thing I just so happened to be standing atop a bleeding werewolf.

I lowered my head and licked up a scarlet trail oozing out of Ransom's scalp, the first sustenance I'd imbibed in nearly twenty-four hours sitting rich and salty on my tongue. The effects, however, went far beyond squashing the low-blood-sugar wooziness in my noggin. Instead, a jolt of energy flowed through me like lightning, empowering my muscles and also providing a sixth sense I'd never experienced before.

Abruptly, I knew exactly where Mama was without needing to twitch my whiskers and make wild guesses. She'd slid lower in preparation for another strike to Ransom's belly. But before she could scratch, I leapt.

I shifted as I fell, landing with arms around my mother's neck as if I was once again a child. And in response, her face materialized before me, so familiar that it seemed like merely a day rather than over a decade since I'd seen her last.

"You're all grown up. My beautiful daughter." I wasn't sure if the words came out of her throat or simply flew into my head without the need for sound waves. Either way, almost-tears squeezed my throat so hard I could barely speak.

"Mama," I whispered after one dry-throated swallow. "You can't do this. You have to *stop.*"

Her eyes met mine, so much like peering into my own reflection that I shivered. Then—long before I was ready to lose her—she was gone, disappearing back into the void from which she'd come.

For my part, I was tumbling to the stage, no longer supported by my mother's barely corporeal body. Was listening to the shifters who—now that it was safe—had converged upon the recent battleground.

"She grabbed herself?" one asked, confused.

"Kitsunes can have two bodies," another answered, seeming sure of something that definitely didn't match up with my understanding.

Then the mutters merged into one endless stream of anger. And the sky disappeared above my head as the pack dove as one on top of my prone and winded form.

Chapter 17

"*Step back, go to your tents, and stay there!*"

The words were clearly an alpha commandment given the speed with which my attackers disengaged from the fight. On the other hand, the alpha tossing around orders was just as clearly Gunner rather than Ransom based on the way my debt tugged at me to follow in the receding werewolves' footsteps.

"I don't have a tent to go to," I muttered under my breath, getting ahold of my body with an effort. And when I was finally able to look around me, I noted that most of the werewolves seemed to be engaged in a similar battle of willpower. Only, in their case, the issue appeared to be whether to accede to the younger brother's wishes...or to continue protecting their wounded pack leader by killing the obvious kitsune in their midst.

Lucinda alone had no such ambivalence about which action to engage in. She picked herself off the ground where Mama had flung her, marched up to Gunner, and slapped him hard across the face. "You *bastard*!" the female hissed. "You won me and now you're angling for fox booty in addition?" Then she stalked out of the amphitheater with a sway to her walk intended to show Gunner precisely what opportunity he'd tossed aside.

And, to be honest, I couldn't really blame the other female for her anger. After all, from what I understood about the battle I'd walked in during, Gunner had as good as taken one girl to the dance then prepared to leave with another. As the side piece in question, I wasn't particularly thrilled.

Ransom was quick to agree with my assessment. "Brother, you have a *lot* to learn about women," the pack leader noted, blotting at his bloody face with the shirt he'd discarded a few moments before. And he looked so prosaic in that moment that I suddenly doubted the instinct that had made me conclude he was the Master. Could Mama really have broken through her minder's magical bonds so thoroughly as to attack him if that had been the case?

"On the other hand"—Ransom's voice broke through my thoughts as his eyes scanned the ambivalent shifters—"my brother speaks for me on matters that don't pertain to women. This fight is over. Now *go.*"

I turned to follow the other shifters, my mind already racing with ideas about how to track down my sister. Because finding her had to be my top priority, even above ferreting the Master's identity out. The guys would have brought her somewhere safe but would have assumed I'd know how to find them. So...

"Not *you.*" Ransom's words, while not impacting my footsteps the way Gunner's had, froze me in place nonetheless. Because what the pack leader might lack in overt dominance, he clearly made up for in wiles....

Only, Ransom wasn't speaking to me. His gaze was instead intent upon his brother, and now Elle was tugging at my arm.

"Mai," she murmured, pulling me along behind her until we stopped in front of a nicely dressed male that I'd met once previously. Was he Lincoln, Leonard? Whatever his name, this was the same shifter who'd slammed the door in my face the first time I'd visited the Atwood mansion, the male who had filled Ransom's goblet while Gunner was fighting...and, apparently, the twin Elle had spoken of so fondly of during our riverside lessons.

Because—"Go with my brother," my mentor murmured before sliding away from me and back toward the sibling standoff. The electricity in the air was raising the hairs on my arms, but she slid between the duo as if there was no danger, removing the shirt from Ransom's fist and bringing the fabric up to dab gingerly at her pack leader's face. "You're going to have a shiner..." she berated him.

Then I was being drawn up the stairs behind her brother, away from everyone I knew within this strangely combative pack.

"I JUST WANT TO FIND my sister," I offered once we were out of the amphitheater and away from the danger Ransom's presence represented. Unfortunately, the male beside me seemed disinclined to offer any direction. Instead, he thrust out his hand in a distinctly unwerewolf-like gesture of greeting.

"I'm Liam, in case you don't remember," he said.

"Mai," I answered, accepting a grip that was firm but not overpowering. Despite the unpleasantness of our initial introduction, Liam seemed less like the stereotypical werewolf and more like his easy-going sister. A definite relief given that he was the sole familiar face in the swirl of werewolfishness that surrounded us both.

"And now I know where Elle's been running off to," Liam continued, his words mirroring my pondering. "I'd thought all the secrecy meant she was stepping out on her boyfriend...."

"Her husband, you mean." I frowned. "Or mate, rather. I thought werewolves chose a partner for life."

"You've been reading too many novels." Something dark and wounded flickered across Liam's face as he answered, then he turned on his heel and led me downhill and deeper into the forest without another word.

So—mates, not a good topic. I grimaced, deciding that holding my tongue was a good decision when faced with a prickly shifter whose sore spots were impossible for a stranger to suss out.

After that, we walked for several minutes in silence, signs of werewolves dissipating until we might as well have been wandering through an uninhabited wilderness rather than skirting around the edges of the shifter equivalent of a professional networking convention. Still, there was no sign of Kira. So, eventually, I caved and asked again.

"My sister..." I started, having to speak up this time to be heard over the sound of a nearby waterfall. Rather than answering, though, Liam held up one hand in a request for patience then pulled me off the deer trail we'd been following and straight through a thicket of thorns.

In a minute, I decided, I'd turn back and find someone more likely to lead me to my sister. In a minute....

Due to the dim evening lighting or my own rushed thinking, I didn't realize we were on a clifftop until Liam paused...then dropped right over the edge. Only when I picked my way to the cliff edge after him did I see that Liam was holding onto the side of the rock face with one hand while leveraging himself down a series of ungainly but apparently human-created steps that led to a flat ledge of rock at the base of a waterfall.

How handy, I noted. *To have a hideaway close to but at the same time unrelated to the gathering....*

The existence of this secluded spot, however, became irrelevant as soon as my eyes drifted down to the cluster of shifters gathered at the shadowed cliff base. Allen, Tank, and Crow were all huddled so close together that I could barely distinguish one from the other. Then a shifter leaned backwards and I clearly saw the comatose form of my sister lying at their feet.

Chapter 18

"**W**hat happened?" I gasped out as I broke into their cluster. Pebbles were still tumbling down the staircase behind me, but I didn't actually remember working my way through the intervening space. Somehow, though, I'd ended up at the bottom while Liam was still nearly at the top. Meanwhile, the roar of the waterfall must have muffled the clatter of my approach because Tank and Crow responded as if I was an enemy, leaping to their feet and arraying themselves protectively between Kira and myself.

Allen, on the other hand, remained seated, cradling the teen's sweat-sodden head in his lap. "She collapsed," he said simply, recognizing me before the others did. Then he scooted sideways and let me take over his position, Kira's limbs flopping doll-like as she was transferred from his embrace to my own.

"No wonder. She's starving and thirsty," I explained aloud, trying not to berate myself for dragging a thirteen-year-old along on a journey that would have stressed a full-grown human. But even while latching onto a rational explanation, I knew there was likely more to it. Because Kira's stamina, until this summer, had been better than that of a marathon-running horse.

"Here." A bottle of water pressed into my left shoulder blade, one of the shifters having come prepared for a thirsty and comatose kid. But I lost track of both bottle and companions as my sister's eyelids fluttered open, the dark orbs below watery with unshed tears.

"Mai?" she whispered, trying and failing to sit up under her own volition. "Ow," she mouthed as she gave up on the motion, falling back against my knee while cradling her own head.

Then two shifters were leveraging her halfway vertical, a third was unscrewing the cap and tilting water between her barely parted lips. The liquid seemed to do the trick, too, because Mai's breath started coming a bit easier, the sweat I wiped away from her forehead failing to immediately reform beneath my hovering hand.

"Do you guys have a granola bar? Some beef jerky? Crackers?" I couldn't quite understand why Allen, Tank, and Crow averted their eyes at this question, so I continued listing what I considered readily available snack food. "Cereal would work also. Or a sandwich. It's been almost a day since Kira ate last."

"You're starving too," my sister murmured, her eyes squinting as if the dusky light of evening was instead the glaring sun of midday. In fact, her words weren't even audible over the roar of the waterfall—I was forced to read the rebuttal in the motion of her lips.

"I'm fine," I promised, placing both of my hands on my sister's shoulders, barely finding a spot around Allen and Tank's supporting fingers and arms. "Well?" I asked again, meeting the eyes of each male, one after the other.

They were silent for one long second. Then: "We don't bring food to the gathering," Allen explained. "We hunt as a pack...."

"Even when there's a sick child who recently fainted due to hunger?" I raised both eyebrows, unable to believe that we'd need Ransom's say-so before giving my sister food.

The guys' lack of answer served as confirmation and I wanted to shake them. But *I* didn't have to kowtow to the Atwood pack leader. Better to solve my problem than to vent my spleen.

So, gently releasing Kira, I rose to my feet and turned back toward the forest. "If anyone wants to help me, I'm going to find food for my sister. If not, I hope you'll at least keep her safe while I hunt."

LIAM WAS THE ONLY SHIFTER who offered to join me, and even he was more trouble than he was worth. Oh, the male willingly dropped his shorts at the cliff top and shifted into fur form just as I did. But every time I thought I was close enough to pounce upon a critter, the blundering werewolf scared my prey into flight.

"What are you doing?" I demanded half an hour later, curling into my human body after a particularly plump squirrel had scrambled away up a tree trunk to escape our approach. I'd lapped up a couple of sips of water at a stream we'd run alongside a few minutes earlier, but I still felt like I could have drunken an ocean and swallowed a whale without stopping. That measly squirrel had looked pretty darn good to me.

Apparently not to my companion. "You want to eat a rodent?" Liam asked, joining me on two feet and standing just a hair too close for comfort. I'd become accustomed to the lupine disregard for personal space while spending time around Gunner and his pack mates, but I was still a little squeamish about having a near stranger—and werewolf—inches away from my unprotected neck.

And perhaps that discomfort is why my words came out sharper than I'd intended. "I want to find something *edible* for my *sister*," I bit out, magic sparkling around my fingertips as my star ball responded to my adrenaline-fueled reaction. Then I sighed, expecting Liam to retreat at this evidence of my kitsune nature.

But, instead, he merely cocked his head and apologized. "I'm sorry. I wasn't thinking. Which way should we go next?"

Liam sounded so much like his twin in that moment that I couldn't hold onto my anger. Instead, I offered an apologetic smile of my own before turning away, scanning our surroundings in search of something small enough to capture with vulpine jaws.

Fresh deer scat peppered the leaf litter beside me, but I dismissed the evidence of an animal far too large for my fur form to bring down unaided. The sulfurous stink of stagnant water from the south, on the other hand, suggested a pond might be within easy walking distance. The evening was nearly dark already...surely birds would now be roosting for the night?

They must be called sitting ducks for a reason, I decided, hunger making my mouth start to fill with digestive juices. Sleepy waterfowl should be well within my abilities, even though I'd apparently wasted my childhood becoming an expert at swordplay rather than learning how to hunt.

"Let's head...." I started, then spun as a strangled yelp emerged from the spot where I'd last seen Liam.

Where Liam still was...only in wolf form instead of on two legs. He wasn't the sole wolf present, however. Instead, another beast had joined us while I was gazing in the opposite direction. Had joined us...and leapt upon Liam as if intent upon tearing out my companion's throat.

Chapter 19

I recognized Gunner one moment before the magically created spear left my fingertips. So rather than skewering my protector, I let the star ball diffuse back into pure magic as it flew toward the battling wolves.

I wasn't exactly sure what I expected to accomplish using incorporeal magic. But I have to admit, the net of blue light that landed atop the duo, yanking them out of their fur forms and back into humanity, was inspiring...and something I didn't think I'd been capable of before licking up Ransom's blood.

Gunner, on the other hand, was still intent upon his aggressions. "Stay away from Mai," the alpha growled out of newly humanized vocal cords. Despite his speech, he didn't appear to realize he was two-legged since his teeth then proceeded to clamp down upon the other male's furless neck.

In contrast, Liam was quick to acknowledge their shared humanity. Perhaps it was the blunt human dentition that tipped him off?

"What's wrong with you?" the slighter male countered, twisting away from his cousin and pulling himself up onto his knees in the process. "I was watching her back, you idiot. You should thank me, not jump me from behind."

I didn't consider myself an expert at werewolf relations, but even I could tell that "idiot" wasn't the brightest word to use around an angry alpha. Sure enough, Gunner didn't respond verbally, the air instead tightening with electricity. It was only a matter of time before he shifted back into lupine form and continued the fight...

...A fight that was delaying Kira's much-needed nourishment every moment it continued. So, rather than letting the males duke it out the way I usually would have, I gave the thread of star ball attached to my fingers another yank and watched the net of blue light around the males' shoulders snuff out the sharp bite of electricity once again.

So this *is kitsune power*, I thought, smugly amused by my ability to manipulate werewolves...

...then my legs collapsed out from under me as the last of my stolen energy fled in a whoosh.

That got Gunner's attention the way Liam's words hadn't. Supportive hands grabbed me one millisecond before my head struck the rocky ground. And even though my eyes were squinted closed against painful dizziness, the scent of dew-soaked granite proved Gunner was once again back in his right mind.

His warm arms enfolded me, pulling me close up against him as he lowered us both onto the ground. "Mai," he murmured, breath teasing tendrils of hair so one flirted ticklishly with my cheekbone. "We need to feed you. Kira is already enjoying roasted deer meat...."

"With Ransom's permission?" I murmured, keeping my eyes firmly closed in an attempt to prevent the world from spinning out of control once again.

"I speak for my brother in all matters that don't pertain to women, if you'll recall."

His words were amused; his smile pressed against my skin like sunshine. *Why,* I pondered into the darkness behind my eyelids, *am I making such an effort to keep this alpha at arm's length?*

"And, on that note, I think I'll head back to the campground," Liam interrupted, reminding us both of his recently forgotten presence. "You can thank me later, cousin, once you're feeling a little more sane."

In answer, Gunner growled, the rumble vibrating through his entire body before entering mine by proxy. His lack of control, however, recalled my own abilities. Unlike prideful werewolves, I knew how to be appreciative of provided help.

So I forced myself to push out of the warm darkness, opening my eyes and turning to meet Liam's gaze before the latter had time to depart. "*I'll* thank you, Liam," I offered. "I appreciate all you've done for me."

And I got the distinct impression that no one in the Atwood pack had ever noticed Liam's behind-the-scenes efforts previously. Because his lips quirked upward on one side and he saluted me sardonically. Then, dropping down into his lupine form, he trotted away into the trees.

"I WISH YOU HADN'T COME."

The warmth in my belly dissipated as Gunner's words hit me like a slap in the face, and I rocked back on my heels to escape from the unexpected reprimand. But before I could think of an audible answer, the fickle alpha had pulled me into the deepest bear hug I'd ever been a part of. And the explanation he whispered in my ear definitely softened the sting of the preceding words.

"You would have been so much safer if you'd stayed put at Wildacres. And yet, I'm selfishly glad to see your face."

Gunner couldn't actually *see* my face at the present moment, not when my cheek pressed into his naked shoulder, one large hand cupping the back of my head. All it would have taken to turn this hug of concern into an actual embrace was the slightest twist to our bodies, an alignment he and I never quite seemed to manage at the same time.

Now, for instance, there was information I needed to relay that trumped the demands of my libido. So I didn't turn my torso toward him. Just drew my head away from Gunner's shoulder sufficiently so I could speak.

"I wasn't trying to come here," I admitted. "At first, Kira and I were just fleeing the wolves who showed up on our doorstep after you left with your brother...."

"Wolves?" Whatever thread of romantic interest had previously been forming between us snapped as Gunner leaned away, his neck bending so he could peer into my face. There was only starlight above us, but I could still make out his pupils, so dilated they looked like caverns I could have plummeted into. I wasn't so sure that, once falling, I'd ever be able to halt my descent.

So I turned away, spoke to the trees as I finished my telling. "Werewolves," I elaborated. "I didn't recognize any of them, and they didn't get close enough for me to smell whether they belonged to your pack or to someone else's. At the time, all I could think about was getting Kira to safety."

Gunner hummed his understanding. "So you decided there was strength in numbers."

"Actually, no." I wished I could have said that my immediate reaction had been to track down my allies and stand united in the face of unknown dangers. But I was still far more of a lone fox than a pack wolf, regardless of my companions. So, haltingly, I admitted the truth.

I told Gunner how Kira's tiredness had spooked me. How I'd lapped up dried werewolf blood then let the tug in my gut lead me here, where dreams of my dead mother suggested the stealer of Mama's star ball currently resided. How I'd tried to contact Mama in the waking world, but had every attempt in that direction resoundingly rebuffed until the big fight in the amphitheater.

I *didn't* tell him who I thought was the culprit, however. Couldn't quite talk myself into hurting Gunner further until I was 100% sure.

"I need to figure out what's going on with Kira, but then I'll get out of your hair..." I finished, knowing the werewolf beside me had unfinished business of his own to tie up and that my presence would only get in the way.

Only, before I could complete my promise, Gunner raised his hand as if to halt the outpouring of words. He wasn't gesturing me into silence, however. Instead, he grabbed the skin of his wrist between sharp wolf teeth, grabbed it and *tore*.

Then, holding the bleeding appendage out toward me, the werewolf beside me ordered, "Drink."

Chapter 20

In the near darkness, the blood sliding across Gunner's skin and puddling in the crook of his elbow appeared black as swamp muck. Unappetizing in color but salty sweet in scent. No wonder my stomach growled hungrily at the sight.

Still, I was more than a mere animal. So rather than licking up the blood the way I'd done atop Ransom's shoulders, I instead peered into the eyes of the alpha who appeared to be offering his own ichor as fuel...for what exactly? Surely it would have been easier to lead me back to the waterfall and provide a chunk of well-cooked meat to satiate my hunger.

"Werewolf blood appears to be a kitsune's turbo-pack," Gunner rumbled by way of explanation. "If that's what you need, I'm more than willing to provide."

The offer appeared to be limited-time-only however. Because, before I could answer, my companion sighed and pressed his right hand atop the wound to slow the flowing blood.

Except, when my eyes managed to leave the tantalizing liquid and instead latch onto Gunner's face, I realized that he was giving me an even greater gift—time in which to think. It was hard, though, to hash out implications when the ooze collecting beneath my companion's fingers drew me as seductively as his kiss had stolen my breath back at Wildacres. Hard to hash out a pro-con list when I could almost feel the power surging through me, the potential so great I didn't know where the limits of werewolf-fueled kitsune magic might end.

I only realized I'd leaned in closer when a stray droplet splashed up to land on my cheekbone. It burned colder than ice...and yet my tongue rather than my fingers licked out to lap at the blood.

What had been frozen agony on my skin melted like chocolate when worked upon by digestive juices. Tensed muscles eased, aching stomach softened. That single drop of blood was as good as chugging a gallon of energy drinks at revitalizing my flagging strength, and my head cleared even as my muscles relaxed.

Which meant I was finally able to speak, even if the words sounded stilted to my own ears. "I don't know what will happen if I accept your offer. For all I know, this would tie us together in ways you might later regret."

"Or it might help you speak with your mother and save your sister." Gunner paused, the hand he had clamped upon his opposite wrist loosening, preparing to once again release the flow of blood. "The future is, by definition, unknowable. But it's better to dive in than to give up."

Bold wolf words, but my fox brain chose to accept them. So, reaching forward, I drew his bleeding arm toward me. Then I dipped my head and sucked his life force in.

MAMA'S FINGERS SLIPPED hair behind my ears as she tugged me away from Gunner. Or was that my own fingers slipping hair behind the ears of my oldest child?

I rose to my knees, lost in the joining. Felt ice suffuse my skin as Mama's dead spirit merged with my living body. Love poured between us, a deluge that threatened my breathing. But why should I even need oxygen if I was a spirit and already dead?

"Mai." I didn't hear Gunner's word at first. Didn't remember it referred to me, in fact, until his bloody hand clamped down upon our—my—forearm.

He smelled strongly of fur, earth, and ozone. Meanwhile, the warmth of his body as he pulled me up against him reminded me vaguely that my heart still beat and blood continued to flow through my veins.

Words cascaded over me, harsh and guttural. At first, they were only meaningless syllables. Then they materialized into a sentence. "Is she there?" Gunner asked.

"I'm here," my mother and I responded together. "He's cute," we continued—or, rather, that was Mama entirely, not me.

I caught the faintest whiff of amusement floating toward me through the darkness. "I'm glad you approve, Mrs. Fairchild," the werewolf murmured, his voice so deep it was almost a growl. "But let's stay focused, shall we? Who is your Master? And what does he have to do with Kira growing more and more weak?"

I whimpered, the agony of Mama wrenching herself from my body hitting me so hard that I barely managed to lunge forward and grab onto her wrist before she disappeared into thin air. "Don't," I croaked, understanding without having to be told that Mama's Master wouldn't allow this line of questioning. Then, in her words: "I can't speak about the Master. Please, don't ask."

"Not even if he's a male or a female? Human or werewolf? Maybe even a fox?"

Shivers racked my body and the pain of losing my mother was so intense I could barely uncurl my fingers. She was almost gone and we hadn't yet found out anything about Kira. So, reacting instinctively, I slapped one hand over Gunner's mouth, not realizing until too late that I was entrusting my fingers to a werewolf's fangs.

"Quiet," I ordered. Or maybe Mama ordered? Because as Gunner's words faded, I once again lost the distinction between spirit and self.

This time, Mama enfolded me from the outside. An icy hug that nonetheless warmed me from head to toe.

Meanwhile, huge werewolf paws rose to move my fingers so they no longer blocked Gunner's nostrils. But my companion remained silent as Mama and I, together, spoke.

"A kitsune can only have one daughter," we whispered. And now I saw images flickering through my mind's eye that I'd never been privy to before. The combined joy and sorrow when Mama realized she was pregnant a second time. Her decision to sacrifice herself to allow Kira to come into existence. I felt the pain and resoluteness as a star ball was wrenched from her own body to give her second daughter a chance at life.

"I gave Kira my star ball to use when she grew older," Mama continued, speaking through my lips. But we were separating now, my own throat aching with suppressed tears as my mother slipped out of my skin and drifted outward until only our fingers were touching.

She couldn't tell us the next part—couldn't mention the shadowy being who controlled my mother's spirit and magic so completely. I struggled to think of a question that would help Kira without eradicating my mother's presence entirely. And as I pondered, Gunner spoke.

"What can we do to keep Kira safe without a star ball?"

"Nothing," Mama murmured. And now her voice was a whisper on the breeze rather than an utterance from my body. "Kira fades as my magic is used elsewhere. Without a star ball, a kitsune cannot continue to exist."

Chapter 21

I swayed, shaken by the realization that my mother had died of her own volition in an effort to keep Kira from doing the same. Nearly as bad was the fact that I'd dropped the protective-guardian ball quite literally. Still, at least I knew how to begin correcting my mistake.

"Whoever bought Mama's star ball must be here at the gathering." In fact, I had a very good guess who the Master might be. I just didn't want to speak the words aloud in front of Gunner until I had more evidence that Ransom was the one with the rotten core. "I just need..."

Gunner cut off my words before I could state the obvious—that I needed to ingratiate myself to the larger group of Atwood werewolves in order to sleuth out the identity of the 'Master.' The werewolf beside me, unfortunately, had a different take on the matter at hand.

"You and Kira need to be somewhere off the radar," he finished for me. "But Ransom will balk at any of us going along to protect you. And we've already discovered that Wildacres isn't as safe as we'd initially presumed...."

His over-protectiveness was sweet in a way, but it also raised my independent fox ruff like nobody's business. "So you want me and Kira to run away while, what? While you do the hunting for us?"

The vision of Lucinda clinging to Gunner rose, at that exact moment, in my mind. Only to be followed by the more realistic image of Gunner trusting his brother, trusting someone who only wished him ill....

I wasn't the only one irritated by our lack of like-mindedness. My flaring nostrils picked up Gunner's burst of alpha aggression, and the loaded silence between us was so tangible I could have cut it with a knife.

Then Gunner—despite being a dominant werewolf used to getting whatever he wanted—backpedaled quite gracefully. "I'm not trying to tell you what to do," he offered. "You're your own woman. I get that. I just want to help."

"So help by telling me what I can do to get a toehold in this pack without compromising my sister's safety," I suggested. "Help by promising that you won't let Kira out of your sight while I'm gone."

I rose as I spoke, my feet carrying me back and forth between the trees that surrounded us. I didn't want to stand here arguing with my supposed ally. Instead, I itched to run back and check on my sister, while at the same time I also wanted to forge ahead and keep Kira from weakening further yet.

Luckily for my patience—or lack thereof—Gunner didn't wait long before he made a suggestion. Apparently the high point of the gathering was a Solstice Hunt, a time to restructure pack hierarchy without killing anything except local wildlife. "You'll be accepted into the pack if you do well in the Hunt tomorrow," Gunner admitted, voice low and reluctant. "But to be part of the chase, you'll have to swear fealty to my brother...."

"Fealty like the oath that sent you to your knees?" A bad idea if the Master really was who I thought he was.

Air currents swirling between us as Gunner nodded rather than elaborating. He didn't have to tell me that a bond like that to his fickle older brother was the height of lunacy for a lone fox like myself.

Or was it?

For one split second, a very different image flitted through my head. Not me submitting to a power-hungry alpha and possible serial killer. Instead, I saw Allen, Crow, Tank, and Elle running beside Gunner in wolf form...with my fox tail leading the chase.

Shaking my head against the daydream, I pushed myself back into the dangers of the present. No, I didn't relish the idea of pinning myself down beneath Ransom's thumb willingly. But if an oath was what it took to save my sister, I'd figure out the specifics on the fly.

"Alright. I'll do it," I decided. "And you'll watch my sister every minute? All of you? Everyone you trust?"

I tasted the electricity of Gunner's displeasure. Smelled his urge to gainsay me, to take over this hunt and manage it on his own terms...or at least send half of his trusted comrades along to guard my back.

But, again, the faintest breeze of a sigh flowed between us. "The pack will meet at dawn on a rounded hill west of here. It's open to the air, grassy. You can't miss the spot."

Of course I couldn't miss it when Kira and I had come from there that same morning. I shivered, suddenly remembering the dream of blood on grass that had been set on a hill so much like that one. Then I shook my head, thinking three steps ahead.

It would take half the night to return to the hilltop. And I needed food in my belly and at least a few hours of sleep if I hoped to win a place in the Atwood pack....

Still I lingered, not wanting to leave while a barrier hovered between me and Gunner. I was shunting the male aside through my own fox nature as much as to protect my sister, and we both knew it. But I couldn't quite turn myself into a wolf and act like any other pack mate.

So—"Thank you," I told him one second before shifting into my fleet-footed animal. But I heard no answer before I lost myself to the darkness of the night.

SITTING DUCKS WERE, indeed, easy to slaughter. Their feathers, on the other hand, took an eternity to gnaw off with vulpine teeth. So I ended up shifting into human form to skin the waterfowl, shifting back to fox form to chew raw meat off bones, then collapsing in exhaustion not far from the spot where Gunner and I had split up.

Kira's court date is tomorrow. I woke hours later instant alertness. And if I'd had human vocal cords to swear with, I would definitely have used one of the words Kira's social worker hated so much.

No two ways about it, I was burning bridges back in the city. And I was running late for my intended goal of making a good impression on Ransom's pack as well.

Luckily, I was a fox and my animal instincts left little room for self-recrimination. Instead, I rose, stretched once to ease aching muscles...then I ran like the fires of hell were licking at my heels.

Kira was right—sticking to the stream made the journey from campground valley to meeting hill far less strenuous. Meanwhile, the dim pre-dawn light was plenty sufficient to let me pick out easy routes I'd been unable to follow with a sick and weary human child dragging along behind. I scampered across a gully on a fallen tree trunk, listening to bird songs growing louder by the second in the woodland version of a bedroom alarm clock.

I was nearly there though. Meanwhile, the howl of excited wolves flowing downhill toward me promised that the pack hadn't divided up into hunting parties quite yet.

So I wasn't too late after all. I wasn't too late...but I wasn't paying sufficient attention to my surroundings either. One moment I was sprinting flat out to join up with the gathered werewolves. The next I was yelping as huge fangs cut into the soft skin of my flank.

Perhaps, I noted even as I spun sideways, *the pack is no more excited to meet me than I am to meet them.*

Chapter 22

O nly, apparently I was wrong. Because even as I twisted upwards and lashed out at the attacking shifter with my newly materialized sword, someone behind my back noted, "Not too bad on the reaction front."

Meanwhile, another voice was less approving. "Still not good enough to be an Atwood wolf."

So I was being judged. Or hazed. Or perhaps there was really no difference between the two motivations. Because the wolf-form shifter in front of me didn't pull his subsequent attack one iota. Instead, he dove under my sword so rapidly that I was hard-pressed to force him back.

Or I would have been hard-pressed had Gunner's blood not fueled my footsteps. As it was, my feet pivoted and lunged faster than I'd thought possible, my muscles flexing even more quickly than kitsune strength should have allowed. Unfortunately, the boost could only do so much against an uncountable sea of attackers.

Because I was no longer facing a single werewolf intent upon disemboweling me. No, there were dozens of ozone-tainted opponents, their sharp scents biting into my skin as I whirled to stab at a werewolf leaping toward my unprotected back.

Instinct told me to play dirty and end this, to lower the odds against me by hook or by crook. To that end, I *could* have twisted my sword to the right and turned a scratch into a serious injury, taking my opponent out of the fight for good.

But, instead, I pulled the thrust after it skimmed epidermis, uncertain whether I'd lose my place in the Atwood pack if I disemboweled one of these wolves. If this was a test, I intended to pass it. Too bad evading my attackers without causing serious injury was akin to fighting with one arm tied behind me.

There were so many opponents moving so quickly now that I could barely make out anything beyond a blur of fur and fangs. Speaking of fangs, one set bit down into my ankle, knocking me off my stride. Instinctively, I pushed a shard of magic out of my sword and into an ankle cuff to protect me. Was relieved when my opponent erupted into humanity, his dull incisors glancing off my skin.

"You bitch," the shifter growled, wiping my blood away from his mouth with the back of one hand. "You'll regret..."

I didn't have time to listen to further recriminations, however. Because the other Atwood shifters were still four-legged, still slobbering with the urge to fight. And they now appeared to be banding together. Joining up into pairs and trios in preparation for hitting me from multiple fronts.

As much as I hated to change my tactics, Kira's face rose in front of my mind at that point. When given a choice between dying or killing, I had to chose the latter for my sister's sake. I couldn't simply surrender and hope for the best.

So I took a deep breath and selected my first quarry. I'd start with the small wolf on my left side, proceed to his partner then work my way through the wolf pack.

Before I could put my plan into action, however, warm skin slid up against my naked backside. Large fingers settled over my sword hand, clenching down and freezing my weapon into place.

Once again, someone had slipped through a gap in my defenses. And this time I was quite thoroughly caught.

"IT'S ME. LIAM," MY jailer offered as I tried and failed to elbow him in the kidneys. Then, when my tensed muscles proved I had no clue who he was referring to, the male sighed and elaborated even as he released my sword-bearing hand: "Elle's brother. I have your back."

Right. My brain unfroze as terror slid off my shoulders. For some reason, Liam's name was eminently forgettable, but I found myself glad that Gunner had disregarded my orders to keep everyone watching over Kira and had instead sent his cousin to ensure I made it through the day intact.

Because it was ten times easier to fend off attackers using teamwork, especially since a flicker of movement out of the corner of my eye promised that Liam had come prepared with a weapon much like my own. For thirty seconds, we both attacked and parried, the yelping of wounded four-leggers proving that my sword mate wasn't being as sparing as I'd been with his slashes. Apparently I'd misunderstood the level of injury allowed within a pack.

"Since when do werewolves carry weapons?" I asked after a few moments, when my panting had eased into regular inhales and exhales. Meanwhile, without looking back over my shoulder, I twisted counter-clockwise to jab at a white-furred shifter who was attempting to sneak up on Liam's right side.

"Since Atwood tempers made fighting in fur form a threat to pack cohesivity," Liam answered, pivoting right alongside me while his words flowed as easily as his sword hand had.

"You're an Atwood? Related to Gunner and Ransom on your father's side?"

I'd meant the questions to be idle conversation, but something about the silence behind me suggested I'd struck yet another nerve. *Yes, great idea. Insult your sole ally*, I berated myself, kicking out at one werewolf while swiping a great puff of fur off the back of another. "I'm sorry," I offered as I riposted. "None of my business. I'm just glad you've had sword training and are willing to help me out."

I half expected that to be the end of our partnership. But, to my relief, the close-mouthed shifter accepted my apology and opened up to me far more than he'd ever done before. "Gunner, Ransom, and I are double cousins," he offered. "Two sisters married two brothers. Very romantic...until you ask yourself who ended up with the consolation prize."

The haze of fur, I noted, now came from my human companion as much as from the werewolves behind us. "Liam..." I started, trying to remember every trick I'd developed to soothe ruffled lupine fur over the last three months spent in wolf company.

But before I could put my new skills to the test, yet another shifter stepped out of the trees beside us. I was half-turned away from him, yet I still recognized the Ransom by his size and bearing one second before the pack leader opened his mouth to berate us.

And despite my best intentions to stand tall, my shoulders hunched against the tongue-lashing I knew would be forthcoming. After all, our brawl had made a significant proportion of the pack—not just myself—quite definitively late. Meanwhile, Liam had just told me that Atwoods couldn't stomach being disrespected....

Sure enough, the pack leader flattened his underlings against the soil in a wordless burst of pure, unadulterated rage. Then, turning to face me—the only one still standing—he demanded, "Why do you disrupt my Hunt?"

Chapter 23

I knew that cowering would have eased the pack leader's displeasure, but a fox can't afford to submit in the face of a larger predator. Instead, I squared my shoulders and stood a little taller. Then I told Ransom—and all of the werewolves arrayed around us: "I didn't come to disrupt. I came to join."

Bracing myself for another eardrum-shattering roar, I was surprised to instead see Ransom's lips curling upward into the same subtle smile Gunner graced me with whenever I fell for one of his practical jokes. Only, the younger sibling had always been laughing *with* me during those past episodes. At the moment, I got the distinct impression I was about to become the butt of the older brother's joke.

"Did you now?" the pack leader purred, pacing toward me and slipping one finger beneath my chin so he could tip my head from side to side until the intensity of his gaze heated my features. "Because my brother couldn't get the job done, eh? Left you cold last night just as he did with Mirabelle and would have with Lucinda had she stuck around to go home with the victor after our little game."

A feminine growl emerged from behind me—Lucinda if I didn't miss my guess. But I was instead struggling against a grin that wanted to split my features. Of course Gunner wouldn't fight to bed a pack princess. But he *would* fight to ensure she

106

didn't end up stuck having sex with some male against her will. The realization that Gunner's actions had been honorable rather than caddish the previous evening made me want to laugh and dance.

"Hmm?" Ransom nudged me verbally, hand still on my chin. And this time I mustered up a jerky nod in response.

"I'm here to join, alpha," I reiterated. And my answer must have been sufficient. Because, releasing my chin, Ransom turned his back on all of us and strode off in the direction from which he'd initially come.

Which left me and the lesser werewolves scrambling to keep pace with their leader, some rubbing shoulders in human form while others slunk forward in the skins of their beasts. Several knocked against my shins in the process, trying to topple me over subtly enough that they could swear the jab had been accidental. But I was too elated to take offense.

Because not only had Gunner been absolved, I'd also succeeded in my mission. I was *in,* and without having to swear an oath to the unpredictable pack leader either. Now I just had to determine whether Ransom was also the Master....

In search of confirmation, I felt for a sign from Mama in my belly, only to be met with complete silence on that front. Not that the Master in question was likely to let his servant off her leash again after such a show the previous evening. Instead, I'd need to use my wits to regain Mama's star ball. But at least I was here in the midst of the action where the solution to the mystery was within reach.

By this point, we'd reached the hill where the Solstice Hunt began and ended, a rounded knoll lit by sunlight that had brightened several lumens past official dawn. The orange on the horizon was already softening into true morning so the mass of werewolves arrayed before me showed up as individuals rather than as silhouettes. There were so many of them, though, and most were strangers. The chances of picking out the Master in this milling crowd of not-quite-humanity seemed far less possible than it had one moment before.

Of course, I wasn't entirely human. So I closed my eyes, pulled up my fox instincts, and proceeded to hunt with my nose.

Because shouldn't the Master smell a little like Mama? If Ransom was utilizing a kitsune's magic, shouldn't her jasmine perfume wreath the pack leader just as it always had my mother?

And, sure enough, the faintest aroma of jasmine drifted in over my left shoulder even as Ransom's voice broke into my thoughts. "I know you're all excited to determine who will serve as my second-in-command for the year ahead of us," he called, proving that he was the kind of leader who liked giving speeches. I wasn't particularly surprised by that realization either. In fact, I was glad of the leeway to squint my eyes more tightly shut and continue working on the tricky puzzle of instinct and scent.

"But we have another item on our agenda before I turn you loose to hunt this morning," Ransom continued. His voice, I noted, was deep and mellifluous when not competing with his brother's. As if he really was a pack leader as long as Gunner wasn't there to throw him off his stride.

Unfortunately, Ransom's pack-leader potential showed itself in more ways than oratory smoothness. Because while I'd forgotten the male's teasing smile, he hadn't forgotten my precarious position here in the territory he commanded.

"Mai Fairchild."

My eyes shot open as my name rolled across the sea of shifters between us. All around me, werewolves murmured, swiveled, turned as a unit to peer into my face.

I, on the other hand, was gazing directly at their pack leader. His lips, I noted, had curled back up into that faint, mocking smile. His neck bowed ever so gently like a king overseeing his subjects. And his words were soft as he told me: "I'm now ready to receive your oath."

Chapter 24

My oath. "I..." I cleared my throat, blinking furiously as I struggled to find a way out of the trap that had closed around me while my attention was focused inward. Somehow, when I'd told Gunner I was willing to swear myself to his brother, I'd assumed I'd think of some clever compromise during the intervening hours before I was forced to actually live up to my boast.

But Ransom's eyebrows rose as he eyed me impatiently. And any ingenuity I might have once possessed refused to show itself upon command.

So, thinking of Mama's recent bombshell and the precariousness of Kira's hold on reality, I accepted the inevitable and took the only path I could see toward my destination. "I, Mai Fairchild, swear to protect and uphold the Atwood pack to the best of my ability...."

The words gushed forth as if they'd been waiting for an outlet for weeks on end rather than being forced awkwardly from my lips by a force greater than myself. I *was* willing to protect the Atwood pack, I realized...at least the portion of it I'd spent the last few months living amidst.

Because Gunner and Tank and Ransom and Allen and Elle and Liam had been more than mere companions. They'd hunted with me and trained me and protected my sister with their lives.

Pack mates. They were pack mates and I was glad to acknowledge that connection with an oath.

And as I spoke, the debt-bound tie that had clenched my gut for months gradually loosened. As if promising to be part of Gunner's pack was all that had been required to allow my first full breath in several days.

For half a second, in fact, I could almost see the younger brother there beside me. Could sense Gunner's delight as he accepted the binding I'd created and offered a similar oath of his own in return.

"I swear to protect you and yours also," the alpha murmured, the warmth of his promise soothing skin pebbled by the morning chilliness. *"I welcome you into our pack."*

Then I was back in the forest, one very unimpressed pack leader glowering down at me from the crest of the hill. While Gunner had taken my oath as a heart-felt promise aimed at a group he cared for, Ransom understood my verbal slipperiness to be a personal affront.

And that was the difference between the brothers, wasn't it? Gunner had no need to make others feel smaller to increase his own stature...while Ransom had literally perched himself on the highest point in the forest in an effort to dominate his clan.

Means, motive, and opportunity. I shivered as the likelihood that Ransom really was the Master punched me in the gut.

But before I could follow that thought path any further, Ransom dismissed my evasion with a curt: "Enough of this." His eyes flashed but his tone remained full and firm as if he'd gotten exactly what he desired when he continued. "We'll meet back here to compare our kills at sunset. Ladies, I assume you want to hunt together. As the weaker sex, you deserve a fifteen-minute head start."

I WOULD HAVE CHAFFED at the chauvinistic send-off if the aroma of jasmine hadn't begun dissipating at that exact same moment. The owner of the scent appeared to be moving away from me rather than standing before me. Which meant...maybe Ransom wasn't the Master after all?

Gladly, I leapt upon any thread leading me away from tying guilt to Gunner's brother. The speed with which the pack princesses fled, however, left me little energy to quibble over who might have spilled Mama's jasmine perfume all over herself. Instead, we were deep in the forest before I caught up to the slowest female, fox agility barely making up for my shorter stride as we pressed through tangles of weeds and bushes as a pack.

Then, finally, wolf tails were slapping at my muzzle, which meant I was close enough to search for the floral odor's source. Not that my fellow runners let me. First a clawed foot struck my eye as I veered away from a thicket of brambles. Then, blinking furiously to regain full vision, I changed my trajectory, was pushed sideways a second time, and realized the females were actively attempting to exclude me from their midst.

Which suggested...they were all in cahoots with the Master? The idea didn't sit right, not when I knew that these females had left several different clans quite recently in hopes of becoming Ransom's designated mate. One *might* be my shadowy nemesis, but the chance that all twenty-odd females were working together to wreak havoc using my mother's star ball seemed so slender as to be nonexistent.

All of these thoughts flitted through my head in the time it took for us to descend a steep hill and start back up the other side. I still smelled jasmine quite strongly—the only reason I hadn't turned around to hunt more likely prey. So, pushing a hair more speed out of my dragging muscles, I leapt onto a tumble of massive boulders that allowed me to cut across the path of the earth-bound pack princesses, knowing even as I did so that I'd have no better luck invading the cluster from the front.

Only, the pack princesses were no longer pressing forward. Instead, as if reacting to an unspoken signal, the triangle of werewolves opened up into a circle at the base of the boulders, the lead wolf trotting backwards to sniff at a newly shifted female lying naked on the earth. The girl—because she probably hadn't yet reached her twentieth birthday—was sobbing furiously. And for a moment, I lost the thread of my thoughts and decided the Master could wait until we discovered whatever had set the poor teenager off.

I was too far away to soothe anyone, but the lead wolf was shifting and pulling the younger woman into her arms already. "Shh, it's alright," Lucinda murmured. Because, of course, the female who had glared daggers at me the previous evening *would* turn out to be the unofficial leader of this temporary pack.

"But it happened *again*." The girl's voice quavered, her tone nasal and rough due to stopped-up nostrils. Meanwhile, my own nostrils flared as I noted the strong presence of Mama's jasmine aroma emanating from the center of the circle of were-wolves.

"Are you *sure*?" one of the other females asked dubiously. But I wasn't really listening. Instead, I'd leapt down from my perch and padded past the milling wolves who were too intent upon the teenager's story to hinder my approach.

Because I had a sinking suspicion I knew what the girl was so upset about. Especially given the evidence of Mama's blood-gathering tactics from my dream....

Sure enough, the child answered with a gesture, lifting up both hands in front of her face palm-sides outward. "There's no mistaking this," she whispered.

And she was right. Because I'd seen those same blood-rimmed fingernails on my own hands when joining Mama's hunt in my dream.

Chapter 25

"**Y**ou need to leave." I regretted the words as soon as they left my mouth. Because I should have been debriefing the child to figure out how my mother had possessed her, should have been figuring out whether there was an obvious connection between the Master and his prey.

On the other hand, I didn't really regret my instinctive re-action. Because this poor child couldn't stay here to be used as some sort of magic-harvesting sex slave without her knowledge and consent.

Only now Lucinda was in my face, her long nails biting in-to the bare skin of my shoulder. "What have you done to my sister?" she demanded, clearly drawing kitsune-related conclu-sions that were more grounded in reality than I cared to admit.

"*I* haven't done anything," I countered, forcing my star ball to remain quiescent despite the danger of two dozen angry werewolves pressing closer and closer upon me. "But it's not safe for her to be here. It's not safe here for any of you."

Because while Lucinda's sister was likely the easiest mark among them, I saw no reason Mama couldn't slip into someone else's skin if her Master so commanded. Even if I couldn't find our shadowed enemy in this cluster of pack princesses, at least I could protect them...and cut off the Master's easy access to werewolf blood at the same time.

And that quickly, Lucinda dismissed me as irrelevant. "Go tell your grandmother how to suck eggs," she rebutted while turning away as if I'd ceased existing. The female dropped to her knees then scrabbled through the leaf litter, and for one split second I thought she might have lost her mind...

...Until a ziplock-coated cellphone emerged from the hole she'd so recently dug with her manicured fingers. "You were right," Lucinda said into the microphone after two short rings ended with the sound of heavy breathing. "I need a pickup."

"You and Gloria and anyone else?" The voice on the other end was masculine, hard—an unhappy werewolf. But Lucinda wasn't cowed. Instead, she raised her eyebrows and surveyed the faces that surrounded us on every side.

"My brother will take anyone who wants away from this shithole," she informed her audience. And, honestly, I couldn't blame her for breaking up what should have been a carefully choreographed werewolf courtship and had instead turned into a frat-boy party minus the beers. Not even when her final words promised Ransom would be raging in the near future: "Who wants in?"

A moment of silence...then the rest of the pack princesses agreed in a flood of relieved acquiescence. To no one's astonishment, Lucinda didn't offer me the same pickup service she'd granted to the others. But, as the other females turned away in preparation to depart, she *did* toss me the powered-down cell phone in a gesture that came very much as a surprise.

"If you have anyone you can call for backup, I recommend you do so," Lucinda told me. Then she, her sister, and the rest of the pack princesses shivered back down to four legs and set off north, toward what I assumed was the closest road.

UNFORTUNATELY, I WASN'T a werewolf with backup waiting. That said, there *was* one loose thread I'd left dangling that could be cleared up with a simple call.

"Stephanie Baumgartner, Social Services," Kira's social worker answered, her voice less effusive than I was used to. But, of course, Stephanie wouldn't recognize this number. Wouldn't know who was calling her out of the blue.

"It's me, Mai," I started before leaving honesty behind entirely. "My phone's battery died, so I'm using a friend's. Guess I wasn't quite prepared for camping after all...."

Thinking of all of the events of the last twenty-four hours that I'd been totally unprepared for teased out a chuckle. And Stephanie softened, laughing right alongside me.

"Well, that's the point of camping," she responded, all grandmotherly wisdom. "It's good for young people to learn there's more to life than the internet. Fish to catch. Naps to take."

"Mm hm," I agreed. So I needn't have worried. My hurried voice mail had done the trick to keep Stephanie happy and Kira's court case on track after all.

But before I could get off the phone, the arbiter of my sister's future continued onward with her litany of summer-vacation perks. "Hot dogs cooked over an open fire. S'mores! I think it's been at least a decade since I've tasted s'mores."

A tendency to ramble was one of Stephanie's few flaws. Luckily, I was able to pull up the mapping feature on Lucinda's phone while half listening and take advantage of the lull to determine where Kira and I had ended up. Unsurprisingly, this vast wilderness turned out to be part of Atwood clan central. If we just walked west far enough, we'd end up in the more conventional settlement most of these shifters called home....

"In fact, I think I'll come up and join you. I've got the afternoon off and need to squeeze in one more home visit before the big day tomorrow. How does that sound?"

I'd already hummed my agreement before I realized what Stephanie had suggested. "Wait...what? No! We'll be back in plenty of time for a home visit. And we're not car camping. You'd have to hike in quite a ways to get to our site..."

"I'm old but I'm not feeble! Don't worry—I can be there before dinner. What's the address?"

I hesitated, imagining Stephanie waltzing up to a werewolf gathering to check how Kira was getting along. It sounded like a disaster, and I wished for the first time that Gunner hadn't been so inclusive about including Kira's social worker in pack events previously.

Because we'd taken Stephanie and her daughter with us to the movies one day. Had attended her youngest grandchild's birthday party with presents in hand. The line between professional and personal had blurred proportionally...which was likely part of the reason Stephanie had gone to bat for us so firmly in court.

Now, though, she'd wonder if I rejected her offer to join us. Would wonder...and might change her tune at the final custody hearing we still had a thread of a chance of managing to attend.

"Mai? Are still there? These newfangled phones have terrible connections...."

"I'm here," I answered, buying just a little more time in which to ponder options. We'd have to set up a fake camp somewhere far from the gathering for Stephanie's own protection. Gunner would be game, I knew that. And he could definitely make things work....

So I caved and told her: "We'd love to have you join us." Then I rattled off the coordinates and hung up the phone.

Chapter 26

Not wanting to tempt my luck further, I re-hid Lucinda's cellphone as quickly as possible before slipping into my fur form and sprinting into the trees. Because if an innocent human was coming to visit this evening, it had become even more imperative that I track down the Master *now*.

Unfortunately, the world was working against me. At first, the diffuse sprinkles making their way through the canopy felt good against my heated fur and the skin underneath it. But then the sky darkened to twilight, and abruptly it began to pour.

So, okay, I'd navigate back to the meeting spot based on landmarks rather than on scent trails. Over the hill behind me, past that gnarled mammoth of a something-or-other tree, then across the abruptly raging creek....

There had been at least a tendril of fur-flavor to the air guiding me up until this point. But now, as sodden branches drooped wetly against my backbone, I was forced to rely on eyesight alone. Turning in a slow circle, I realized I had no idea where I'd ended up.

Because the map on the phone had made the green blob of wilderness appear not much larger than my neighborhood back in the city. On the ground, however, the forest felt like an inimical being intent upon swallowing me whole.

In fact, I was almost certain I recognized the tree dominating this small clearing. Wasn't that the same gnarled monster I'd passed by when scrambling up the scree slope on the other side of the creek earlier? Either I was walking in circles or....

I padded forward, reaching out one paw to tap at what should have been wet, scaly bark. Only...there was nothing there to pause my forward momentum. Nothing to prevent me from losing my balance and falling forward into the space where my eyes said a tree should have been.

Ice enfolded me. Darkness surrounded me. And when I pulled desperately at my star ball...I found only a weak spark of magic willing to answer my call.

Hopping backwards, I fell over my own four feet in a desperate attempt to escape the illusion. And now that I wasn't in the middle of the magic, I could pick out a shape where the tree had previously stood.

A shape...who turned as I watched materialized into a slender, Asian woman. My mother, or at least a fragment of her through which raindrops continued to fall.

"I'm sorry," Mama mouthed. *"He made me do it."*

Then she wisped into nothing just as a wolf stepped toward me out of the trees.

HE. Of course the Master was Ransom. I wasn't sure how I could have doubted my initial supposition, despite the thread of jasmine leading me away into the female subpack. Not when Mama had as good as pointed me at the clan leader the moment I stepped out of the woods and into the amphitheater.

Not when Ransom himself had proven his sliminess every time we'd had a chance to interact.

Sure enough, the wolf stalking toward me now was rain-drenched but still distinctly cinnamon, the distinctive Atwood streak forming white eyebrows on his lupine forehead. Meanwhile, his ozone aroma carried toward me so strongly it proved the wolf wasn't a run-of-the-mill member of the pack.

Ransom had been clever, using my mother's magic to find and weaken me as I ran alone through the forest. But even though the playing field wasn't exactly level, I was glad of any shortcut that helped me fix Kira's problem now.

In other words, I was ready for our final showdown. So, rather than backpedaling away from the animal who was twice as large as I was, I pushed everything I had into one shift back to humanity. Then I sent my star ball fluttering toward my fingers to turn into a sword.

Only no weapon materialized. No magic remained to be called upon. Instead, the effort left me bent over and gasping for breath.

The wolf, meanwhile, strode steadily forward across the clearing. Wet leaves squished rather than crunched beneath his feet as he advanced. He raised his chin to inhale, then his jaws gaped open as if he couldn't wait to feel my skin sliding beneath his fangs.

What would happen if the Master bit into a kitsune? Would I become bound to Ransom like my mother was, forced to obey his every command?

Now I did backpedal, fingers trailing across the leaf litter as I crabwalked backwards away from the menacing shifter. *Ah, there.* A rock the size of a duck's egg. Rounded and hard, it fit in my palm and flew smooth and true toward my opponent, who was now no more than ten feet away.

I was already turning and running when a human voice erupted behind me. Didn't understand that the tone was high-pitched female, in fact, until I was already twenty feet into the sheltering trees.

"What's *wrong* with you?" Elle demanded. She'd caught up to me already, was slinging me around to face her while her left hand pressed against her streaming nostrils.

My wide eyes and raised brows must have said everything because my mentor's tone softened. "I thought you recognized me...."

"I thought so too," I murmured, adding up two and two and getting twenty-nine and a half. Of course Elle's wolf looked a lot like Ransom's. Because if her twin was the brothers' double cousin then Elle shared the same genetics...and the same likelihood of her wolf possessing red fur and white brows.

"Look, I'm sorry," I continued, struggling to keep my legs from folding as adrenaline left me. That last shift had been a doozy and I suddenly wasn't sure I could do anything until I rested and ate.

"It's okay." Elle brushed off my apology almost curtly, un-worried about both the blood slowly dripping from her nostrils and my lack of further explanation. Clearly she had something else on her mind.

"Mai," the other female started, and I swallowed, not wanting to hear the rest of her sentence. "Your sister didn't wake up this morning. Gunner sent me to find you. He wants to give her blood."

Chapter 27

The forest was so much harder to walk through two-legged, with neither shoes nor clothes to protect sensitive human body parts. Still, it wasn't pain that raised my blood pressure. Instead, the infuriating part was my mentor, who turned out to have been keeping secrets from me all along.

"So you knew I could use werewolf blood just like you could use kitsune blood," I stated, pausing for only a second to pry a minuscule thorn out of the pad of my big toe before pressing onward after my companion. "How could you not mention that when Kira got sicker and sicker? Didn't you think it might help?"

"I wouldn't say 'help' exactly," Elle countered, leaping over a fallen tree as agilely as if she was still in wolf form. I didn't realize how much I was dragging until I tried to follow...and had to sit down on my butt then swing my legs across rather than risk falling flat on my face.

"Ignore the semantics," I ordered, hating the fact that exertion made my voice uneven. "Why didn't you tell me there was an easy way to tap into the powers you were supposedly teaching me to harness?"

I was breathing heavily now, and not just from the effort of bushwhacking. No wonder Elle glanced back over one shoulder, her lips pursing the way mine had done when Kira slicked up her hair into a mohawk ten minutes before we were due to leave for school one day last year.

"Because there are implications," my companion told me after one moment of loaded consideration. "I showed you how dangerous it is for your blood to fall into the hands of a werewolf. When blood flows the other way, between a werewolf and a kitsune, bonds are formed that might not be productive. Which is why I told Gunner to wait before doing anything rash with Kira."

Her words made sense...but they didn't entirely salve my disappointment. Because I'd thought pack mates trusted each other, and Elle had treated me with a distinct lack of trust.

Still, her knowledge was all I had to go on at the moment. And Kira had to be in bad shape for Gunner to send Elle out to track me down in the middle of the Solstice Hunt....

"We're almost there," the female in question promised, as if sensing my worry. Sure enough, the sound of a raging waterfall had overcome the residual dripping of rain off tree leaves. "Can you feel them through the pack bond?" she continued. "That's how I found you...."

And I *could* feel something. A warmth from in front of me, a vague indication of direction. So that's how Elle had managed to appear just as the Master's trap snapped shut. I supposed pack was good for something after all, even if it didn't provide the unconditional support I'd initially supposed.

"I'm actually surprised the rest of them haven't shown up already," Elle rambled, filling the uncomfortable silence that had fallen between us with a steady flow of words. "We went looking for you at dawn, but it was pretty obvious where you were once you tapped into the pack network...."

"The rest of them?" I interrupted, a shiver running up my spine as I realized my sister wasn't encircled by the handful of watchful werewolves I'd imagined. "Aren't Tank and Crow and Allen protecting Kira?"

Elle didn't turn back to face me this time, but I still sensed the reproof in her voice when she replied. "*Gunner* is protecting Kira. Everyone else went out to find you. And...here we are."

Here we were indeed. At the top of the same steep path Liam and I had traversed the night before, the rocks looking even more treacherous wet than they had in the dim light yesterday afternoon.

But the slick stones weren't what provoked a gasp from my companion. No, it was the sight of the alpha werewolf beneath us, blood dripping from his mouth as he hovered over the supine body of my sister. Matters, it appeared, had advanced in a direction neither Elle nor I had anticipated while we were gone.

Chapter 28

lle realized what was happening before I did. "No!" we shouted in tandem, tumbling down the path so quickly I barely felt the stones slicing into my left foot's instep.

At the bottom, I hurled myself atop my sister to protect her while Elle hung upon Gunner's non-dominant hand as if preventing him from throwing a grenade. Only when I saw the blood welling up between her fingers did I realize what was going on.

Gunner wasn't trying to harm Kira. He was trying to help her. And his cousin was intent upon preventing the alpha from carrying out his humanitarian task.

"Mai?" Kira's reedy voice was nearly inaudible. And yet, the evidence that she'd regained consciousness still stopped the scuffle in its tracks.

"How are you feeling?" I demanded, rising so I could press my wrist against her forehead. The guys had rigged a canopy out of tent canvas and arching sticks, so the rain shouldn't have soaked her the way it had me. And yet, Kira's skin was cold and clammy, as if she'd run hard in the winter cold then chilled down without bothering to towel off.

"I'm..." Whatever lie Kira had intended to tell me was cut short as she began to cough. Deep, racking quakes shook her body for so long I could hardly bear it. And when she finally spluttered into silence, Elle released her cousin's hand.

"I still think it's a bad idea," my mentor whispered, as if we weren't all shifters and able to hear her as easily as if she'd spoken at full volume.

Only, we weren't all shifters. Or at least, Kira didn't appear to have caught the murmur. Instead, my sister nestled into my side the way she had as a toddler, wrapping both of her arms around my naked waist. "I don't feel so good, Mai," she murmured. Then her eyes closed as she drifted back into sleep.

I stroked her hair gently, even though, to all appearances, Kira was no longer conscious enough to feel the soothing gesture. And as I petted her, I couldn't help wondering when the strands in question had stopped being smooth and glossy. Had Kira been fading for months without me noticing, or was the Master only now sucking out her magic the way he had mine when I stumbled into that illusory tree?

Feeling the brittleness of my sister's body, I was more than willing to accept Gunner's offered strength no matter what the consequences. Elle, on the other hand, continued to harbor second thoughts.

"If you do this, there's a good chance whoever has the other star ball will be able to manipulate you," Elle argued in a hushed whisper. "And you know you're the shepherd of this clan."

"I'm not the pack leader. My brother is." Gunner spoke the words not as if he really meant them, but as if he'd said them so many times before that they came out by rote. And yet, the whole time, his gaze never left mine. The decision, he was telling me, was in no one's hands but my own.

I swallowed, weighing two bad outcomes. I'd sworn to uphold the Atwood pack...but my deeper allegiance lay with my sister. And even though desperation never led to smart choices, no other solution came to mind.

Meanwhile, Kira turned fitfully, her breath catching in a moan that jabbed at my stomach. Her vitality was slipping away so quickly, I wasn't sure there'd be anything left if I went off to hunt the Master a second time. No, we needed to solve this now...or at least delay Kira's deepening malaise.

So, even though I knew I'd regret it later, I met Gunner's gaze directly. Then I dipped my chin into a nod.

ELLE DIDN'T STAY TO watch the bloodletting. Instead, she muttered something about gathering up our pack mates then picked her way back up the slope nearly as quickly as she'd run down.

Which left me and Gunner to get blood out of his wrist into my unconscious sister, a task that wasn't nearly as easy as it had initially appeared. In the end, I was forced to suck up the liquid and dribble it between Kira's lips mouthful by mouthful, Gunner holding the child's lax body upright and rubbed at her throat to prompt her swallow reflex.

But the transfer, though slow and messy, worked admirably. A pink flush returned to Kira's cheeks within seconds. And as a bonus, the bits of blood that seeped into my own system rekindling my magic as well.

I only realized how pale Kira had grown, in fact, once her lips were no longer purple. And this time she curled into my lap like a sleeping child rather than like an invalid ready to collapse for good.

Gunner's blood wasn't a permanent solution, but at least we'd bought a pocket of breathing room. And I used a few of those precious moments to share information—and suppositions—with the alpha who had so willingly risked himself to give my sister a new lease on life.

"I don't want the culprit to be Ransom," I concluded at the end of a rough rundown of the morning's happenings. "But I think he really might be it."

Because Gunner's brother was a slimeball. Mama's hints led me directly to the male time after time. And, not only that, the elder brother had a supreme motive to delve into kitsune blood magic—he needed a dominance boost if he hoped to truly rule the Atwood pack.

Beside me, Gunner sighed and let his neck bend until his forehead rested on one upraised kneecap. "I don't want it to be Ransom either," he said after a moment. "But I wouldn't be entirely surprised."

And then, finally, he told me the story of Ransom's mistake.

Chapter 29

Ransom and Gunner were inseparable as children. Their father was a traditional pack leader—strong, gruff, and apparently incapable of softer sentiments. Their mother died when they were young, after which they largely raised themselves.

Ransom was the more dominant sibling. After all, one year makes a huge difference when you're five and six, respectively. The older brother coaxed Gunner into crazy adventures that became crazier as the pair grew older. Somehow, though, they always managed to get the aftermath cleaned up before their father found out.

"Until I turned eleven, that is," Gunner told me. Without me noticing, he'd scooted in closer so Kira draped across both of our laps, my stroking hand slipping off my sister's hair to tease the fabric covering Gunner's thighs. He didn't seem to notice, but I might as well have stuck my finger in an electric socket for the way the near-touch sent tremors racing up and down my spine.

"What happened when you turned eleven?" I asked. The rain had stopped, but the day was still far too cool for summer. I tried to tell myself the urge to lean into Gunner's side was just exhaustion combined with the appeal of his furnace-like body heat. But even in my head the argument sounded an awful lot like a lie.

"When I turned eleven, Liam and Elle came to visit," the werewolf beside me rumbled. And, as if it was nothing, he reached over to tuck my head into the hollow beneath his shoulder. I think I lost a sentence or two as I melted into his body, but then the story caught hold of my interest once again.

Gunner hadn't known about this particular set of cousins, so the two strangers invading clan central came as both a surprise and a delight to him. The twins were almost exactly his age and were even more like-minded than his sibling. He spent hours showing them every secret he and his brother had ferreted out.

"If I'd been a little older, I would have understood that Ransom felt slighted by my changing loyalties. I would have included him in our adventures even when he told me he was busy with twelve-year-old things."

I shivered, suddenly not wanting to hear where this story was going. But Elle was now Ransom's favorite cousin. How badly could the childhood misunderstanding have played itself out?

Plenty badly, as I soon discovered.

One morning very much like this one, Gunner woke before dawn to find his brother's face looming over his in the dark. The older brother's eyes were wide, his body soaked as if he'd just stepped out of the shower. "Let's go hunting," Ransom whispered.

Gunner—young, innocent, glad of his brother's attention—willingly agreed.

It was afternoon before the rest of the pack found them. A hot, sweltering humidity had pushed the two siblings to shed their fur after sating themselves on the fawn they'd chased down and eaten two hours earlier. So when wolves raced out of the forest toward them, they just assumed the crossing of paths was coincidence.

But the adults didn't pass by and go on about their business. Nor did they shift back to two legs and speak. Instead, neighbors and relatives acted like strangers, herding Gunner and Ransom back toward clan central in a forced march that lasted the better part of an hour.

There, Gunner was shunted off to the kitchen where his twin cousins picked at cookies and pretended not to worry. "What's going on?" he whispered once the pack second had retreated a few steps to guard the open doorway.

Liam shrugged. Elle's lip quivered. But their throats remained mute.

Time stretched out after that the way it does when you're a child. Gunner wasn't sure if he and his cousins waited for ten minutes or ten hours. All he remembered was straining to hear the raised voices coming from the pack leader's study, being unable to make out words but catching the angry tone well enough.

Eventually, the meeting disbanded. Peering around the legs of the pack second, Gunner caught a glimpse of his brother slinking out of the office on two legs. The twelve-year-old's body was covered in scratches, his eye black and his nose dripping blood. He looked like he'd fought in wolf form and lost, but his spine was straight and his raised chin was proud.

Then Gunner's father was the one emerging. The pack leader marched into the kitchen and dismissed his second with a jerky nod that sent all three youngsters cowering backwards. Despite being Gunner's father, the alpha wasn't the sort of relative you could confide in. At that moment Gunner wished very much that he'd been raised by the aunt and uncle who were spending the summer in clan central along with their kids.

This time, though, Gunner's father managed to look almost approachable. He crouched down until he was several inches lower than the seated children's head level—a very unalpha-like thing to do. Then he placed one large hand on each twin's knee and looked directly into their eyes.

"I'm sorry, children. You may not have known this, but your mother was very sick. She passed away during the night."

Elle inhaled the tiniest gulp of air as if someone had punched her in the stomach. Liam remained stoic as an Atwood male was expected to be.

"Where's Uncle Lucas?" Gunner demanded, suddenly feeling the need to protect his cousins. He straightened and glowered as if he had a chance in hell of staring his father down.

"He went home. He's mourning. You two will stay with us until he's better."

And that, apparently, was the end of the matter. The pack leader left. The twins collapsed into a heap of sobbing. And for the first time Gunner felt like a third wheel in the face of their obvious need for each other and equally obvious disregard for anybody else.

The children had been locked into the kitchen this time, the pack second having stepped outside and closed the door in the face of the children's audible grief. But Gunner knew every secret passage in the sprawling mansion—or, rather, he knew every servant's passageway left over from when the property had been owned by humans rather than by wolves.

So he padded over to the pantry and closed himself into the darkness. Then, feeling his way past huge chest freezers and shelves of non-perishables, he yanked open the small door at the other end and slipped up the stairs without bothering to turn on a light.

The visitors were staying in a suite on the third story, one room for the twins, a bathroom, then another for their parents to share. Gunner had intended to invade their territory and find something that would soothe his cousins' anguish. Maybe a stuffed animal, if Elle still slept with one. Or the locket his aunt had always worn on a gold chain around her neck.

But the suite smelled strange when he entered. As if someone had gone hunting then nestled into their sheets without bothering to wash away the blood. Curious, he crept past the twins' bunk beds and hesitated outside the door to the bathroom.

Only to hear voices from the hallway. "Clean it up," the pack leader growled. Not wanting to be caught where he didn't belong, Gunner opened the bathroom door and slipped inside...

...where he faced his aunt's body splayed across the tile, her skin torn as if a wolf had lit into her in a rage. Congealed blood splattered every surface, the rusty red stark against the bathroom's white tiles. This was no slow slipping into death as his father had suggested. This was clear evidence of foul play.

And premeditated action in addition. Because what were the chances of the horror happening in the bathroom if someone hadn't been concerned with the eventual cleanup?

Not wanting to look, Gunner had nonetheless leaned over to see into the shower. There should have been blood specks on the interior just as there were on the toilet and mirror.

But the white ceramic surface was as pristine as ever. Clean, slick...and slightly damp.

Chapter 30

"**R**ansom killed her?" I didn't even realize I was speaking until my words broke through the horrifying picture my companion had painted.

Gunner nodded, opened his mouth to elaborate...then our secluded niche by the waterfall erupted into a maelstrom of wolves.

They were *our* wolves, though. I could feel it even without trying to pick out individual aromas. Tank, Crow, and Allen being herded along by Elle in her Atwood-marked fur body. All of them shifted upwards in synchrony just as they came level with me, Kira, and Gunner. And at that moment, my sister finally woke up.

"Ew, gross!" The teenager pushed away with so much force that my torso slammed backwards, only Gunner's fast movement preventing my head from cracking open upon the rocks. "Clothes, dudes! How many times do I have to tell you we're not all werewolves? Put on some *clothes*!"

And *that* was the Kira I was used to. Bossy, annoying, and totally uninterested in the reality of situations beyond our ability to control.

Only, apparently, the guys had come prepared for Kira's sensitivities. Because Allen merely laughed, turning around to dig through a waterproof bag I hadn't noticed tucked up against the cliff face. "We've got clothes...."

Predictably, Kira wasn't satisfied by this hopping-to. Instead, she placed her hands on her hips rather than covering her privates, looking as wolf-like as any of the males when she barked out: "I don't want to see your ugly butt! Point that thing the other way!"

Whatever further insults the teen planned to fling in Allen's direction, however, were cut short when a lump of awful, puce-covered fabric slapped her in the face. A flurry of similar soft missiles slammed into the rest of us one after another. And when I glanced down at my own wad of fabric, I saw that Allen had come prepared with one-size-fits-all jogging pants and t-shirts, the latter with unique sayings lettered across the front.

"I love Goofy?" I asked, unable to prevent myself from reading my shirt aloud.

"Cute and cuddly," Gunner noted, eyes on his own pink shirt that boasted a white kitten with brilliant blue eyes beside the three curlicue-laden words.

"They were cheap," Allen countered...then ruined the assertion when the corners of his mouth started twitching. "Or, at least, I thought of you when I saw them...."

If our shirts were the buildup, I had a feeling Kira's was the punchline. So I turned back toward my sister, then paled as I caught a glimpse of Tank's torso seconds before "Lawyers have feelings too...allegedly" covered up the majority of his bare skin.

The joke was borderline funny, but the scratches covering his chest and shoulders were far too familiar. Scratches so much like the ones I'd seen beneath our shared fingers while harvesting blood for the Master with my mother. Scratches like the ones Lucinda's little sister must have left to end up with blood beneath her nails.

I would have liked to think Tank had gotten stuck in a briar thicket to end up with so many skin abrasions. Unfortunately, the evidence pointed elsewhere. Our loyal pack mate was loyal no longer, not after suffering a run-in with my mom.

"STEP BACK!" I DEMANDED, pushing myself between the source of danger and my snickering sister. Unfortunately, Kira failed to hear me as she pranced forward to engulf Allen in a full-body hug.

"I love it! It's perfect!" she emoted, twirling around to show off her t-shirt...which I didn't bother looking at since the girl's motion also sent her closer and closer to the scratched-up werewolf that the Master could now manipulate on a whim.

I wasn't fast enough to prevent their paths from crossing however. And Tank was oblivious to the danger he represented. His face crinkled up into a smile as Kira sprang from one werewolf to the other. Then the girl reached out to smack Tank in the chest...

Only, seconds before her fingers touched, the male's eyes reddened, his muscles tightened. His hand reached out even as my sword materialized one moment too late....

"Tank, *move away from the child!*" Gunner's words snapped over us harsh and sudden as a horse whip. And I felt my sword drifting downwards even as Tank scrambled backwards as if he'd been slapped.

So maybe the Master didn't have as much control over the wolves Mama harvested blood from as I'd imagined? Or perhaps those scratches really had been made by thorns and I'd just imagined the redness of Tank's eyes?

I wasn't yet up to speaking in full sentences, unfortunately. Instead, I finally succeeded in angling myself into the gap between Kira and Tank that I'd been going for from the beginning. Then I leveled my sword against the latter's shoulder, holding him away from my sister while letting Gunner do the talking for us both.

Luckily, the alpha understood my reasoning as easily as if he possessed telepathy. "What's with the scratches?" Gunner asked, his voice rougher than usual as he joined me in a solid wall separating Tank from the rest of our pack mates.

For his part, Tank's brows furrowed, his voice tentative as he angled his neck down so as not to provoke further attack...or perhaps to make 100% sure my sword wasn't pressing in through his flesh. "The story isn't really appropriate to tell around ladies..." he whispered, the husky words nearly as loud as a shout to my hypersensitive eardrums.

"Tell us anyway," Gunner countered.

So Tank did, offering a tale pretty much like I'd expected. One of the pack princesses—no he didn't remember her name—had come on to him this morning. She was cute, willing. "A vixen," he started. Then, his eyes flitted toward me as he realized what he'd said.

I would have laughed at the kitsune faux pas if the stakes hadn't been so serious. Instead, I told Gunner: "We can't trust him around Kira." Then, with my eyes, I added an extra message: *If Ransom is trying to turn your most loyal werewolves against us, you can't keep supporting him the way you have in the past.*

In response, Gunner closed his eyes as if he'd heard my un-spoken addendum. Then he nodded, twisting his shoulders so he was speaking to the entire pack.

"Elle, Crow, and Allen—I need you to move camp and sug-arcoat our situation for the social worker. Tank, you and I have a bear to kill."

Chapter 31

"A bear?"

I wasn't sure if Gunner had turned metaphorical on me, or if he really was planning to shunt off his responsibilities and join in the Solstice Hunt after all. But I had no time to pin him down on the subject. Because the alpha was spearing his pack mates with a gaze that sent them tumbling to their knees one after the other.

"Trust *no one* who isn't here beside you at this moment. Protect Kira to your last breath. Feed her blood if she weakens. Keep Mai and the social worker safe also. Swear it."

Gunner's demands came out in a staccato that peppered his underlings like bullets. They were so cowed, in fact, that no one managed to speak until their alpha provided a verbal nudge.

"Allen?"

"I swear, alpha."

"Crow."

"I promise."

"Elle?"

"I will, Gunner. You know I will."

"Mai?"

I didn't realize Gunner had planned to include me in the oath-taking until his dark eyes turned to grab my own. And, for the first time in living memory, I felt fully caught by an alpha werewolf's stare.

"Mai?" he repeated when words failed me, this second speaking of my name somehow releasing my muscles so I could turn and take in the werewolves gathered on either side of us.

Allen, Elle, and Crow were encircling my sister now, enfolding her within their pack as easily as if she was a pup and they were warriors. Tank, in contrast, waited five paces distant, his head averted as if he was afraid to even glance at the youngster he threatened due to the scratches on his back.

Gunner was taking all of the danger with him and leaving Kira with twice the protection she truly needed. Which meant there was only one way to respond to the question in his sienna eyes.

"Kira will be fine without me," I noted as easily as if naysaying an alpha werewolf didn't make my throat tighten and my muscles quiver. "I'm going with you to hunt this bear."

TO MY SURPRISE, GUNNER shrugged then nodded before turning to face Allen as if I hadn't just disagreed with him when he was in full-on Scary Alpha mode. "Any bears that need killing?"

"Actually, there is one." A cell phone tumbled end over end as it flew between us, Gunner's large palm snatching the device out of the air then tilting it so I could take in the screen.

"Bear eats toddler. Authorities left scrambling," read the headline. Below that was a grainy image that might or might not have been a wild animal.

"Are...?" I started, still not understanding why it was worth tracking down dangerous wildlife today rather than tomorrow.

But Gunner shrugged off my half-question. "Can you carry this in your magical pouch thingy?" he demanded, the words sounding strangely official in his deep, gravelly growl.

"Sure," I agreed, twisting my sword into a fanny pack even as the phone was handed off to me. Then, with no time wasted on farewells, Tank and Gunner were lupine and running, my fox form having to sprint to keep up.

Just like before, branches lashed me in the face while wet mud slipped dangerously beneath my paw pads, leaving me little energy to worry about my sister or wonder about bears. Instead, I just ran. Behind Tank, before Gunner. My speed slowing the pack who likely could have covered ground twice as quickly if I hadn't been in their midst.

Despite my shorter legs, however, we were all panting equally by the time we stepped out of the trees at the edge of what had to be the Atwood clan home. It looked like a settlement in suburbia, all rocking chairs and flowers. But the air smelled of ozone and wolves.

And no wonder, because a pup no larger than a house cat slid out an open doorway seconds after we stepped onto the pavement. I didn't know werewolves came in sizes that minuscule. But, oblivious to its puny status, the youngster yipped in excitement...then ran straight for Tank.

I shifted and lunged, half expecting the Master to somehow sense the opportunity to wreak havoc upon wolves his brother cared about. But Gunner was there and grabbing the puppy before I could insert myself between them. The alpha opened his jaws wide enough to fit the youngster's head inside, lowered his eyebrows, roared...

...And the puppy laughed in counterpoint. Or it barked out what passed for laughter in a young werewolf, wriggling its plump body and wagged its tail uncontrollably.

Only then did it leap out of Gunner's grip and into the arms of a female I hadn't even noticed approaching. "Is the hunt over?" she asked, her eyes hooded with worry even though she barely spared a second glance for the pup. "Is Marcus alright?"

"Your mate is in perfect condition," Gunner answered. "But we're hunting bear...."

The female, apparently, understood the implications of that sentence where I didn't. "Then you don't want to walk through town and be bombarded with questions. Here, let me grab my keys."

Clutching the puppy closer, she speed walked back up to her residence. Took, apparently, one moment longer than necessary because Tank shifted to join us two-legged, reached out to grip his alpha's bicep. "You trust her not to send someone to warn your brother?"

"Becky is my third cousin. She won't break."

Of course, Becky had to be *Ransom's* third cousin also. And what did bears and brothers have in common anyway?

Then the female in question was back, pup absent but keys dangling from outstretched fingers. "Marcus's SUV has four-wheel drive. It'll get you wherever you need to go. There's emergency gear and clothes behind the back seat..."

"Thank you," Gunner answered, cutting into her refrain. Still, he wasted one moment stepping forward and bending his head down to kiss her on the forehead. In a millisecond, Becky's stringent scent sweetened as worry slid off her shoulders, proving that the tall, broad Atwood before me was 100% pack-leader material.

He might be pack-leader material, but his role wasn't yet official. And that, I gathered, was why we leapt into the vehicle and drove off in search of a bear.

Chapter 32

"Alpha, may I speak?"

I'd never before seen Gunner's inner circle so tentative around him. But I wasn't entirely surprised by Tank's behavior either, not after Gunner had nearly bitten off his head when the lawyer made the egregious mistake of...offering me the passenger seat. Tank probably had no idea why the scratches on his shoulders meant he was no longer trusted to sit or stand behind me. Sometime soon, I'd have to pull him aside and clue him in.

Not right now though. Because Gunner was growling permission for further conversation even as he steered us off clan central's small gravel driveway and onto a paved, two-lane road. Pressing hard on the gas pedal, he zipped up to and past the speed limit in a matter of seconds. Then, when Tank still hesitated, he bit out: "Speak."

"Yes, alpha." Tank's eyes were firmly focused on the cell phone I'd handed over after we all shifted, and not due to his usual internet addiction either. Instead, I got the distinct impression that the male was submitting in the only way possible before a stronger werewolf whose behavior was even more terrifying for apparently lacking cause.

Without thinking, I reached forward and placed four fingertips against the lawyer's neck by way of consolation. And, wolf-like, Tank relaxed on an instant, flashing me a grateful half-smile before finally spitting out what he had to say.

"It's your prerogative to change your mind, alpha. And I'm not saying it's a bad idea to go after the bear. But last week, you told us you had no plan to challenge your brother. So we don't actually know where this animal is located. Perhaps it would be simpler to skip ahead to the sword fight...."

"No." Gunner's negation pushed me and Tank back in our seats as admirably as if he'd accelerated the vehicle. Noting our reaction, he smoothed out his tone as he explained: "Ransom deserves the chance to step down gracefully. Proving prowess at a hunt worked at deciding dominance between our father and our uncle, and it will work for me and Ransom as well. We'll find the bear."

The highway we were on reached a T then, and Gunner turned left without bothering to pause at the stop sign. There were no other vehicles around to make the traffic violation dangerous. And yet, the motion sent a spear of agony cutting through my head.

Pressing my fingers against my temples, I murmured, "Wait...."

My words were too quiet to impinge upon the loaded conversation taking place in the front seat. But as the SUV began accelerating, leaving my stomach behind at the crossroads, I realized what my body was trying to express.

We're going the wrong way. Yes, that was the problem. So, forcing a little volume into my voice, I added: "Turn around."

I didn't expect them to listen. Not when the pair's current conversation was loaded with implications, weighed down by

Tank's scratches and whatever difficult brotherly decisions were flowing through Gunner's head.

But the alpha heard me anyway. Slammed on the brakes. Then made a U-turn that depended rather strongly upon Becky's promised four-wheel-drive feature as the passenger-side wheels ended up in—then out of—the ditch.

I barely felt the bumping beneath me, however. Instead, my breath was coming faster as I reached forward to tap Tank on the shoulder. "The phone..." I started.

Then the device was in my hand, the news article I'd only glanced at previously filling the screen. The image was somehow clearer than it had been previously, as if I was present there in that secluded residence by the photographer's side. There was blood on the animal's hind leg, I noted. Had it cut itself breaking in?

And suddenly I was consumed by the bear's body. Was stomping through leaf litter, heavy pads and thick claws scraping against rough rock.

Slinging my weight around, I didn't spare a thought for predators. Instead, when I smelled the stink of a weasel, I merely laughed....

Then I was back in my human body, my head so light and dizzy I felt like I hadn't eaten in three days. "He's to the west," I noted. Then, rolling down the window, I vomited up my guts.

"NO," GUNNER GROWLED.

"Yes," I answered.

"Save me from lovers' squabbles," Tank muttered. "If you two keep arguing, we won't get back before dark."

I sighed and tried to get a stronger hold on my temper. On the plus side, my first merging with the bear's consciousness had been enough to guide us toward a dead-end road at the edge of a vast wilderness area. But my magic was too weak to allow for a repeat of the endeavor. And Gunner stubbornly refused to allow me to boost the signal by consuming Tank's blood.

"You'll drink mine," the Atwood leader repeated through gritted teeth that appeared to be sharpening. But I'd drunk from Gunner multiple times over the last twenty-four hours. And, from what I'd read between the lines recently, he planned to kill a bear singlehandedly, drag it back to the meeting hill, then possibly fight his brother—to the death?—in an effort to wrench control of the Atwood pack out of Ransom's hands. I didn't particularly want to weaken him with a third bloodletting if there was another willing werewolf on hand.

I didn't say any of that, however. After all, I'd been around werewolves long enough to understand the alpha's well-deserved pride.

Instead, I started spinning half truths. "If I drink from Tank, there's a good chance it'll break whatever hold the Master has over him," I guessed, hoped. "It might..."

Gunner stepped forward so abruptly my subsequent words lapsed into breathlessness. "You want this?"

"Yes." I barely had breath enough to reply.

"And you're willing?" This to Tank.

"Of course, alpha."

"Then do it." Only, Gunner didn't stand aside and let Tank slip in between us. Instead, he crooked his finger, waited for his underling to approach, then reached down to encircle the latter's broad wrist in his even larger hand.

Gunner's fangs bit into Tank's skin so quickly I wasn't the only one left gasping. But the lawyer stifled his inhale, closed his eyes, and made no complaint as Gunner lifted the open wound up to my lips.

The gesture felt strangely intimate. And at the same time exactly as it should have been. Me, Gunner, and Tank united within our own small pack.

But the blood on my tongue was bitter, so acrid I almost spat it back out rather than swallowing. This experience was nothing like drinking from Gunner. Instead, it took all I had not to push Tank's wrist away.

Nonetheless, the rich blood strengthened me. I could feel it infusing my star ball with a burst of power, hooking me back into the mind of the bear....

"Come," I whispered around Tank's bleeding body. Only, it wasn't me speaking. For half a second, I felt Mama's fingers on my shoulders. Warning, warming.

Then the blood slowed, sweetened. And I knew that the bear was much closer than I'd initially thought.

"Watch out!" I yelled, not minding the way words came out along with a spray of bloody spittle this time. Because the killer bear was right behind Gunner. Had gotten its wires crossed and decided werewolves were just as easy prey as the average pint-sized toddler.

Meanwhile, my warning had turned Gunner's attention toward me rather than toward the massive animal. So I could do nothing but watch as it reared up to slash at his back.

Chapter 33

Gunner shifted and twisted as the bear fell forward on top of him. Which didn't mean he came away unscathed, of course. But at least the bear's tremendous claws merely swiped a gash from furry shoulder to billowing ribcage rather than ripping the wolf's belly all the way out.

No wonder the bear roared out frustration at losing such an easy kill, its breath wafting over me in a vile wave that overwhelmed my senses despite the distance between us both. The stench resembled fly-covered carrion and sleepless nights spent ruminating, telling told me even better than the newspaper article had that this bear was the animal version of a serial killer, less interested in eating than it was in the kill.

I noted all this in the time it took to call my sword into existence. Even magical steel seemed too soft to pierce a bear's thick hide, actually. But I had to at least try to tilt the battle in our favor....

Except, Tank's hand swung down out of nowhere, pinching my fingers so abruptly that I reverted to mistakes of a beginner, dropping my blade as if my fingers had become coated in grease. The weapon flashed into pure magic as it left me, slipping around my ankles and melding back into my skin for later utilization. So I hadn't lost the potential for swordsmanship. And yet....

"What the...?" I demanded, whirling and peering into Tank's face. I expected the flash of red promising the Master had taken control of his senses. But, instead, the lawyer's eyes were as blue and clear as water reflecting the sky.

"No weapons," he explained tersely, his hand still clenched down on mine as if to ensure I listened. He spoke as quickly as if the judge had offered him a mere ten seconds for his summation. "That would be cheating. They'll check the hide for signs of gun or knife wounds. Which isn't to say Gunner can't have help in fur form from a second and a mate...."

Mate. The word left me speechless long enough that Tank had already shifted and dove into the fight before I came back to my senses. Now would have been a good time to retreat to the vehicle. But, instead, the pair flanked the bear from opposite directions, lunging forward so quickly the behemoth was hard-pressed to keep up.

That was our opponent's weakness, I gathered. Size meant it lacked both speed and agility. Still, the wolves were making little progress, their teeth sliding through fur without leaving blood trails behind.

And they were already wounded, both of them. Gunner now suffered slashes on his muzzle and hindquarters matching the one the bear had swiped across his side at the beginning. Meanwhile, Tank looked little better, with a wound on his temple that had barely missed taking out one eye.

Eyes. Of course. The bear's skin was impenetrable to the efforts of a wolf pack. But a fox might be able to run up its back and strike the animal blind....

Moving as quickly as the thought occurred to me, I was four-legged and fleet-footed in the time it took for Gunner and

Tank to choreograph yet another attack against our shared enemy. The bear had previously seemed bamboozled by similar joint efforts. But this time, it ignored Gunner and swung at his companion, flinging the lawyer against a nearby tree so hard that he didn't even manage to yelp.

Move, Tank! I screamed silently, hoping the lawyer would manage to regain his footing before the bear lumbered into a charge. Unfortunately, Tank lay still and silent...and then I lost sight of him entirely as I clawed straight up the bear's body, clinging to its matted fur.

The beast shivered like a cow shaking a fly off its hindquarters, but otherwise seemed rather uninterested in me as I clambered up. Cresting its spine with little effort, I came to rest on top of its broad head just as the beast rose two-legged above Tank's comatose body....

Meanwhile, Gunner was nipping wildly at the bear's hind legs beneath us, attempting and failing to reach the softer skin of the animal's belly. Not that even a bite there would have halted the upcoming carnage. Because the bear's fur was even thicker on its underside, hanging down in long, tangled sheets.

And then it was time to put my plan into action, despite the stench so foul it nearly made me lose my grip. I braced my hind legs and leaned down to go after one beady eyeball, each orb as brown and liquidy as the next.

At that moment, however, Tank whimpered, coming awake just in time to see death looming above him. It wouldn't be *his* death, though. Not if I could help it....

I strained with all my might to reach the bear's eye without losing my footing. Then, just as I slashed, the pupil flashed bright red.

Chapter 34

So Mama summoned the bear after all, I noted even as the possessed animal beneath me twisted faster than a bear really should have been capable of. It flung me off its forehead and toward Tank, and all I could think was: *I failed my pack.*

Air pressed my fur against the skin underneath it, and I braced myself for impact with the surrounding brush. But it was human hands not hard wood that hit my body, human hands that grabbed my feet and boosted me back aloft.

Because my pack had felt me coming. And somehow Tank had understood my game plan well enough to fling me back into the exact right place.

I hit the bear's neck faster than I'd left it, scrambled upward even as Gunner nipped wildly at our enemy's flesh. Predictably, the bear lashed out at him, dinner-plate-sized paw extended...and this time Gunner didn't even try to dodge our shared enemy. Instead, he latched down on the soft skin between already bloodied claws, giving me time to complete my attack.

It was too late to gamble on a paw stroke, not when Gunner was already deeply entwined with the bear's claws. Instead, I dove at our opponent's eyeball, biting hard just as Gunner was doing down below.

The orb popped like a grape, but I had no time to be disgusted. Just scooted sideways to take out the other eye even as the bear raised both front legs to paw at its streaming face. Then I leapt free, barely making it off the toppling bear before being crushed beneath its descending body....

Because wolf teeth apparently *are* sufficient to tear out bear bellies. Or at least they are if the bear in question is blind and unable to fight back. Tank and Gunner were soaked in blood and half-digested intestinal contents before they finished. But all I felt was sublime relief.

Relief that even though Mama had obeyed the Master and drawn this bear here as ordered, she seemed to have been looking out for my best interests after all. Because now we had the means necessary to win Gunner's ascendancy to the head of clan Atwood. As long as we arrived back at the meeting hill before dark, that is.

Unfortunately, the sun was falling quickly toward the tree line, the hard work of rolling the bear carcass into the back of the SUV taking all the strength we had left. Wordlessly, we tumbled into the vehicle, Tank in the front and me and Gunner in the rear cargo area. The alpha pulled the scariest-looking hunting knife I'd ever seen out of the bag that had yielded up our clothes earlier, hacking into the animal's hide as he explained: "We'll bring the head to prove our kill...."

Despite the grisly spectacle, I felt safe beside my pack mates. And I must have fallen asleep for a few minutes after that. Because when I next looked up, we were turning back onto the gravel driveway that led to clan central. Daylight was fading, the sky burning with oranges and pinks as we rolled toward the street where we'd initially picked up this borrowed vehicle.

We'd need to run to get to the meeting spot by the deadline. A tough sell while carrying our macabre—and heavy—load....

Only, time wasn't the only factor working against us. Because Tank swore from the front seat, prompting me to half rise so I could peer out the windshield.

And what I saw there had my hand falling down to clamp upon Gunner's shoulder in search of reassurance. The quiet cul-de-sac we'd left a few hours earlier was no longer empty. Instead, Becky must have tattled on us. Because the tarmac was covered with what looked like an army of none-too-pleasant werewolves.

Chapter 35

Fox instincts can sometimes kick in at the most inopportune of moments. Like now, when the SUV screeched to a halt and a shifter I'd never before set eyes on stepped forward to pull the hatchback aloft. He and his comrades pressed inward, their scent of fur and electricity invading the vehicle quite thoroughly despite their two-legged stature. And all I could do was struggle against the imperative to shift into fox form, wriggle through the merest sliver of elbow room, and make my escape.

Because I was trapped. Stuck in an unyielding metal box while surrounded by werewolves. I knew it was a bad idea to don my fur and show how different I was from the others, but somehow that knowledge felt distant and vague....

Then Gunner's arm settled across my shoulders, his mere presence thawing the chill in my blood and settling my mind. "Edward," he greeted the closest werewolf.

Gunner's tone was cordial but his muscles were rope-like with tension as he angled me behind him. And even though the posturing of a dominant werewolf goes a long way, I wasn't so certain even Gunner could overcome all fifty of these werewolves while cornered in the back of the blood-stained vehicle....

Tank must have jumped to the same conclusion I had. Because I heard the creak of his door opening behind my left shoulder, then I smelled the lawyer's aroma drifting closer as he padded around to stand at the other werewolves' backs.

So we were three against fifty rather than two against fifty. Somehow that knowledge wasn't enough to soothe my racing heartbeat. Still, I held onto my human skin with an effort, not wanting to make matters worse by giving in to fox terror and skin.

For thirty long seconds, we stayed there, lost in some silent werewolf battle of willpower. Then, finally, Edward answered Gunner's greeting. "Alpha," the former started, dropped to one knee outside the vehicle, his gaze falling so rapidly that his chin thunked against his chest. "Pack leader. We've come to help you carry your kill."

Oh. My breath wheezed out far too loudly, but no one paid me any attention. Instead, the wave of kneeling swept out on both sides from its epicenter around Edward, until the sensation of pack surged up to surround us in a solid wave.

We had backup. I hadn't realized how little I relished the notion of Gunner standing alone against his brother until what seemed like two-thirds of the Atwood clan transferred their loyalties without even being asked to do so.

But Gunner didn't accept the offer as easily as I would have done. Instead, he hopped down out of the vehicle, resting his hand upon Edward's shoulder. And he waited for nearly a minute until the older male lost his fascination with the pavement and finally glanced back up.

"It's dangerous to take sides at this moment," the alpha warned his supporter. "If Ransom wins, you lose quite severely."

"It's more dangerous to be governed by the wrong pack leader," Edward answered just as carefully. And I could read between the lines that he had much more to say.

But there was no time to discuss repercussions and loyalties. Because the sun was dipping below the tree line. Time was running out even as a dozen hands pressed me sideways so they could reach the bear carcass in the back of the vehicle.

Being werewolves, they had no respect for my personal space. Nonetheless, I only had eyes for one werewolf: Gunner.

The younger brother looked so much like an alpha at that moment that it was hard to believe he'd allowed Ransom a shot at being pack leader. And if he was finally going to meet his destiny, I couldn't let my kitsune nature hold him back.

So: "Go. I'll follow," I told him, an unspoken understanding flowing between us.

Then, with a nod at two werewolf strangers who were clearly expected to stay two-legged alongside me, Gunner and his pack mates were running with the bear body between them away into the descending night.

THEIR PATH WAS EASY to follow, the mass of wolves and two-leggers having broken branches and matted down tangles as they arrowed directly toward the meeting hill. But I couldn't shift in front of strangers. So, two-legged, our journey turned into a slow and frustrating slog.

Night had nearly fallen by this point, which was maddening since each flashing lightning bug not only reminded me that Gunner and Ransom would already be meeting...it also made me shiver at the memory of my dream. Blood on the hilltop, me facing the Master directly. If that was to be the culmination of this evening, I wished we could fast forward ahead directly to the end.

But my human feet could only walk so swiftly. And as I opened my mouth to see whether the werewolves beside me might consider shifting and going ahead without me...someone stepped toward us out of the trees.

I didn't realize who it was for ten long seconds, my star ball gathering invisibly between my clenched fingers as I peered into the shadows beneath the pine trees. Was it worth revealing my kitsune nature to fight off this newcomer? I couldn't be sure, but I was ready to do whatever was necessary to ensure I made it to Gunner's side intact.

Only, before more than the hilt of my sword had materialized, Liam stepped out into the open. His eyes were wild as he ran both hands through already ruffled hair, and he barely gasped out "Kira needs you" before stopping to catch his breath.

"How did...?" I started then shook my head at the irrelevancy of asking how Liam had managed to track me down in the vast expanse of forest. He'd likely used the pack bond just like his sister had. And if Kira needed me...then I'd just have to send these two strangers to help Gunner in my place.

"Go," I told them, wishing I could remember the names they'd offered when they'd introduced themselves. But Gunner's furry tail had been receding into the treeline, and their names had gone in one ear and out the other as I stared at their alpha's back.

Now, the pair stood with furrowed brows and cocked heads, unwilling to either obey or gainsay me. We were losing time to their uncertainty, so I reached out and gestured at Liam. Surely the alpha's cousin was a more than acceptable bodyguard....

And, after one glance shared among themselves, the taller shifter shrugged, the shorter one nodded. Then they were dropping into wolf form, sprinting into the darkness, leaving me and Liam entirely alone.

Well, alone save my imaginings of what might have sent Liam running to find me when a succession battle was also taking place in the forest. "Where is she? What happened?" I demanded.

"This way," Liam answered, leading me beneath the glowering bulk of the pine tree from which he'd emerged and away from our fellow shifters who were likely already out of earshot as well as sight. It was pitch dark beneath the needled behemoths, hard for even shifter eyes to capture enough light to walk through. So I wasn't surprised when the male beside me stumbled, his toe seeming to catch on an upraised root.

I grabbed Liam's arm to keep him upright, felt his weight cave in on me as he barely managed not to fall. Yesterday, I would have been daunted by the sensation of a werewolf impinging upon my personal space. But, today, I understood what it meant to be part of a pack. So I gave Liam my strength willingly, accepting his hand as it searched blindly for my own in the dark.

"Ah, there we go," Liam murmured. And he no longer sounded breathless and weakened. Instead, the words were strangely smug even as pain shot through my index finger.

I tried to look down to see what had pierced my skin, but the forest was fading away around me. For an endless second,

I floated in darkness...then I was seeing through someone else's eyes on an all-too-familiar hilltop that was already saturated with blood.

Chapter 36

The blood wasn't human, however, as I realized when the hands I was guiding—broad, callused, not my own—helped three other shifters heave the skinned bear carcass over onto its front. Beside it lay a twelve-point buck, hefty and impressive but no match for the dead predator Gunner had brought back.

So this was what the brothers had been doing while I was trailing along behind them at a snail's pace—butchering recently slaughtered animals to make sure there'd been no foul play. Inside me, hope kindled. I wasn't too late to help the younger brother after all....

Meanwhile, my mouth spat out words both deep and masculine. "No sign of weapons," I growled.

On my left side, Edward dipped his head in a wordless nod of agreement. Immediately, three other shifters followed suit, an impartial jury facing the Atwood brothers and preventing further bloodshed from coming to pass.

Or, at least, that appeared to be our role. Liam was having none of it.

"But the bear's head is separated," Liam continued, pushing the words into the lungs of the male whose body I possessed no matter how hard I tried to bite my tongue against the admission. "Anything could have happened in the neck area. Stab wounds. Gunshots. It's impossible to be certain. This isn't a definitive wolf kill."

Behind my back, I could feel the quiver of dozens—hundreds?—of werewolves reacting to my assertion. Some smelled interested, like spectators at a ball game. Others exuded hunger, the bear and deer apparently having become more appetizing now that they had been thoroughly skinned.

Most, though, were tense and worried. An occasional murmur broke through the constant shuffle of human and lupine bodies, suggesting that the majority of the crowd didn't want this showdown to turn into a physical fight.

Liam on the other hand, was itching for bloodshed. I could feel his excitement quivering beside my real body, could feel his smug pleasure as he guided me up on the meeting hill. More blood meant more power for him. And wasn't the oft-overlooked cousin, even more than the legitimate pack leader, likely to benefit from an upheaval within the hierarchy of the Atwood clan?

I didn't think Liam was actually controlling his cousin, but Ransom was quick to jump into the presented gap. "You think that's all you have to do, eh, brother?" he growled. "Kill a bear, throw it at my feet, steal away the clan I've been raised to lead since birth." Then Ransom's tone smoothed as he recalled his ace in the hole. "Well, I won't let you. Gunner, *I remind you of your oath.*"

I held my breath, expecting that to be the end of it. But the compulsion had no effect on the younger sibling. Instead, Gunner merely shook his head before speaking. "My strongest oath is to this pack, Ransom. Again, I ask you to step down."

So Gunner's obedience in the past *had* all been stagecraft, even down to kneeling in front of his supposed pack leader in Wildacres' mud. Which should have meant the wolf I was backing had the advantage. Unfortunately, his younger brother's lack of obedience only enraged the weaker of the two contestants.

"You won't accept that I lead this pack by birthright?" Ransom ground out, only to be interrupted by a succinct history lesson.

"Our father was the younger brother," Gunner countered, "but the better shepherd of this pack."

"Or so we've been led to believe." Ransom spat, the gob of spittle barely missing his brother's bare toes before joining the bear blood puddling atop the soil. And behind me, the werewolves on the eastern side of the knoll erupted into grumbles that seemed fated to turn into snarls.

So that was where Gunner's supporters had gathered. I wished I was able to turn the neck of this borrowed body to make a count of how many shifters were for and how many against the younger brother....

But I could feel Liam's hand around mine back beneath the pine trees. Could feel his fingers squeezing, pressing blood out of the pinprick while I made no motion to get away.

Not for want of trying; that part goes without saying. But I could do nothing about either my own body or the one here on the hilltop. Instead, without my permission, the latter's feet were already beginning to move.

"Quiet," Gunner chided his followers even as my host body slipped back behind the first row of shifters, using their bulk to shield me/him from view as we padded silently around to

the right. I didn't know where Liam was sending us, but I had a feeling it wasn't anywhere good....

Meanwhile, Ransom seemed to have decided he was a comic-book villain. Because rather than resting upon his laurels, he continued to speak.

"Our uncle was a pushover and a cuckold," the older brother proclaimed, the crowd quieting as the family's dirty laundry was aired in public view. "Why do you think his wife was murdered?"

"You mean why she *died*," Gunner interjected, reaching forward to grab his brother's shoulder so hard the latter's flesh turned red, then white. Why would Ransom want to tell this story when he was the villain? Gunner apparently felt the way I did, but the older brother was unwilling to be shut up.

"No, I mean our aunt was *killed* in cold blood," Ransom countered, shrugging off his sibling's hand and stepping forward in a werewolf display of dominance. "Our father slept with his brother's woman. And our half-brother was the one who snuffed out her traitorous life."

Chapter 37

"Half-brother?" Gunner asked, his voice confused and faltering. *Half-brother*, I echoed inside my own mind. No wonder the bitter jealousy had built up within Liam so profoundly that it brought us all to this point.

Meanwhile, beneath the pine trees, Liam quivered at the revelation of his history. And for half a second, I thought I might be able to rip myself free of his grasp.

But then something warm and moist covered my bleeding finger. Pressure came, a mouth sucked.

I nearly vomited at the knowledge that Liam had taken my digit into his mouth and was even now lapping up my magic. And at the same moment, Ransom clarified his earlier words.

"Liam killed his mother in a fit of jealous anger," the pack leader elaborated. "Did you really think our father and aunt did the dirty in our mother's home only once?"

As that particular bombshell hit, I lost control of the body I was sitting in entirely. Became a passive bystander as borrowed male feet carried me the rest of the way around behind the brothers until we stood only eighteen inches from the pair's backsides.

Then I turned my head—or, rather, Liam turned it for me—noting that the few shifters here on the wrong side of the hill could see little with the moon still hidden beneath the curve of the earth's horizon.

Even as the secrecy of our position sank in, my sword materialized in dark silence. Its hilt fit between the possessed male's fingers as if he was as good a swordsman as I was. Meanwhile, his body shivered as I realized what Liam had brought me here to accomplish.

Gunner! I yelled...or tried to. But the body I possessed just stood stoically silent while everyone around us leaned forward, taken in by the telling of the previous generation's tale.

"...clan or a reality TV show?" "...don't blame him." "...should have known better..." The whispers rose up on every side, and Ransom waited out the reaction. Perhaps the older brother had the makings of a pack leader after all.

Because it was the younger brother who spoke quietly but intently, impinging upon the whispers and adding fuel to the fire. "But you were there. The shower. The hunt. The fight with our father," Gunner protested.

"I came to speak to Elle, found something horrible, and stayed to protect her," Ransom growled. "Our *sister* would have shattered if she knew what Liam was capable of. I thought you understood that. What did you think? Did you think it was...me?"

This was their final chance for reconciliation. Before me, I could smell Gunner rewriting the past and hoisting his brother back up onto a pedestal. And Ransom—even that power-hungry shifter softened. The straight line of his shoulders slumped slightly and his aroma sweetened as the duo hovered on the brink of brotherhood once again.

But that wasn't what Liam had brought us all together for. Instead, back beneath the pine trees, my body turned colder as the Master literally sucked up another healthy dose of my magic. Then, on the hilltop, the softness around the older brother dissipated. The chance for reconciliation fled.

"I see what you think of me," Ransom growled, mind changing in an instant. There were scratches on his shoulders, I now noted. Many of them, both healed and unhealed. As if Liam had wanted to be entirely sure his hold on the older sibling was freshly consolidated.

"Brother," Gunner started, only to be interrupted.

"There's no point in talking."

"The bear," Gunner countered. "Tradition...."

"Are you really so weak that you're afraid of a true contest?"

Even then, Gunner tried to argue. But before he could force out another sentence, I felt my own arm rising. Saw Ransom's body mimic the action. Felt the sword leave my fingers and turn one complete revolution before it thudded into his hand.

For his part, Gunner's head turned not toward the threatening werewolf beside him but to look over his left shoulder. To see the source of the weapon that was now beginning to glow.

Just like the possessed male's eyes would now be glowing. Just like my own eyes might be glowing back in that pine grove.

Because I wasn't just a passive bystander, I gathered. Instead, I felt my training and magic merging together to guide Ransom's fingers even as his brother mouthed my name soundlessly into the air.

"Mai..."

His disappointment was palpable. But there was no time to wallow in the alpha's regret over my actions, because Ransom was already surging forward into an attack.

Chapter 38

The brothers were better matched than I would have expected...especially with my training coming along for the ride on Ransom's sword. In fact, we might have ended the contest prematurely had Tank not stepped forward out of the darkness to hand the younger brother an entirely corporeal weapon that otherwise closely matched my own.

"First blood," Gunner suggested as he hefted the weapon as easily as if it was an extension of his body. And the first clang of blades sent a jolt of electricity up my spine.

This was *wrong*, having my magic diverted from my body. Even worse, though, was fighting against a werewolf I'd come to accept as a member of my pack.

I had no say in the matter, however. Instead, when Ransom started falling for a feint that would have left him wide open, I felt my sword obey my thoughts rather than his muscles, slipping sideways until it once again met Gunner's blade.

The clang was deafening. Gunner's disappointment in me almost as audible. And, as the last sliver of sunlight slipped beneath the horizon, Ransom finally deigned to speak.

"I told you this was no game, brother. We'll fight until there is only one leader left to rule this pack."

Rustles and murmurs from the crowd faded into stillness. I could now see nothing, my sword having muted its glow in the interest of stealth.

"Our father taught us..." Gunner countered. But then he gave in to the inevitable as his opponent pushed forward in a flurry of blows that left no time for further talk.

It was too dark to make out every thrust and parry, but I could feel the first time Ransom's blade cut into his brother's skin. Because the blood surged through me like a sugar rush, making Liam laugh back in the pine grove while my borrowed body on the hilltop gleefully tapped its feet.

Ransom wasn't the only one making contact, however. The air was now redolent with freshly spilled fluids, and the rich tang of immediacy promised most of the scent came from shifters rather than deer and bear. Every second, the metallic aroma grew stronger...and that wasn't the only danger Gunner faced.

Because I smelled the audience pressing in closer as loyal werewolves considered diving into battle in support of their respective alphas. The pack would be physically decimated if they fought each other—I knew this. Worse would be the lack of unity that would ripple outwards to take over the entirety of the clan.

"I, Mai Fairchild, swear to protect and uphold the Atwood pack to the best of my ability...." My oath reverberated in my ears, chattering the possessed male's teeth together painfully. But there was nothing I could do to stop the carnage. Nothing except stand there in the darkness and wait out a battle I couldn't even see.

Then, before me, a pained shriek and a thud as one of the contestants fell earthward. I strained against the bonds that held me stuck in this immobile body, needing to know who had been vanquished and what I could do to help.

"Eh, eh, eh," Liam warned back in the pine grove. He was watching as avidly as I was, I gathered. Was waiting to see how the battle would turn out.

Meanwhile, around my borrowed body, the audience fell silent. It was almost as if only two shifters stood there rather than two hundred or more.

"It's no loss of face to surrender, brother." The victor's voice rose through the air so quietly I wouldn't have heard him if I'd been one row deeper amidst the avid watchers. But I was inches from the combatants, and I almost collapsed in relief at the gentleness of Gunner's tone.

The battle was over and the proper brother had been triumphant. I had one millisecond to relax before Ransom refused to submit.

"Never," the older male started. Then, louder: *"To me! Kill the imposter! Attack!"*

His words were terrifying in both their strength and their purpose, the alpha compulsion crackling outward across the crowd. Feet shuffled as shifters fought against an obviously inappropriate order. But werewolves were hardwired to obey their alphas, and soon I felt shifters pressing against me upon three sides.

The first was already pushing around my unmoving body in an effort to follow Ransom's order when Gunner finally opened his mouth and spoke. *"Stand down,"* he said both calmly and sadly, the two words enough to freeze the entire crowd mid-stride. Then, in explanation: "Atwoods don't fight amongst themselves. Not now, not ever." Never mind that he and his brother had just engaged in an ill-fated battle of their own.

Immediately, the scent of embarrassed submission rose along with a burst of flashing lightning bugs, the insects so bright that for one split second they illuminated the scene. In the light, I saw Ransom kneeling, held in place by the sword poised against his jugular. Meanwhile, Gunner stood above his vanquished older brother, my magically created weapon dangling laxly from his left hand.

And as dark descended around us a second time, the audience reacted to the scene as much as to Gunner's command. "Alpha," some murmured. "Pack leader," whispered others, a growl of agreement rising from those who hadn't spoken yet.

They were pack-oriented and that should have been the last of it. The brothers had fought and the proper alpha had won.

Only Liam wasn't ready for the battle to be over. *"Now,"* he murmured back in the pine grove. And, all around me, shifters lunged toward Gunner en masse.

Chapter 39

The pack was splintering as I stoody by and watched it happen. Then I wasn't watching but was instead joining in the fight...on the side that was not my own.

Because Liam had been around star balls long enough to know that I could draw the blade containing my magic back to me using pure willpower. And as the hilt snugged into the palm of the body I borrowed, my feet carried me across the intervening space and toward the male who had recently held my sword.

I felt rather than saw Ransom roll away between us. Smelled rather than saw Gunner ready himself for my attack.

Back in the pine grove, my stomach roiled with horror. I was about to strike the werewolf who had been nothing but kind to me. I was able to eviscerate my pack mate....

There on the hilltop, however, my hand remained steady. Even in darkness, I could gauge the distance between us through memory of recent sight.

I whirled to come at Gunner from an unexpected direction. Raised my star-ball sword then slashed downward where his neck ought to have been...

...Only to be halted by a flicker of starlight.

No, that was Gunner's blade, parrying. My sword screeched like claws on a chalkboard as it ran up my opponent's. But, at the hilt, it was forced to stop.

Relief flooded me...but not for long. Because my borrowed body was already disengaging and regrouping, making my real body pant in horror as my limbs turned weak. I'd nearly broken something precious in the previous moment. And no matter how much I tensed my real muscles, the ones Liam controlled geared up to do it all over again.

"Kill him," Liam whispered in my ear back in the pine grove.

Meanwhile: "Mai," Gunner breathed toward me out of the dark.

Beside my real body, the Master snickered, a low harsh sound that felt like sandpaper running over my skin. The darkness was Gunner's only real advantage...that plus the fact that he had no reason to do anything other than run away from me. But the alpha didn't retreat. Instead, he as good as painted a target on his chest as he continued speaking.

"You don't want to do this." The words weren't a question. Instead, they were warm and sweet as chamomile tea.

But, heartening or not, Gunner's speech served to locate him in the darkness. And once again my magical sword thrust forward, this time angling to slide through my opponent's ribcage and into his heart.

Somehow, though, Gunner managed to turn at the last instant so my blade cut through nothing. The lack of contact knocked me off balance so I faltered, misstepped, almost fell.

"Our *pack*." The alpha's whisper caught me as ably as physical hands might have. Set me back on my feet even as they filled my brain with an idea. Was he suggesting...?

"A pack is only as strong as its weakest member," Liam interjected, speaking through me. Our shared voice was cold now. Angry. Intent upon Gunner's death.

And just like that, my sword began glowing like a beacon. Claws scratched on hard earth behind me. A bark morphed into a growl. The magical light was attracting Gunner's enemies. It would only be a matter of seconds before I'd feel the hot breath of werewolf hunger flowing across my skin.

"If you can't do this, I will," the Master warned. *"You'll like my solution even less."*

Without me willing it, my head turned back to glance behind me. A dozen red-tinged eyes materialized behind my back. These wolves would tear Gunner apart in seconds, would skin him alive and laugh as he screamed.

Gunner must have sensed the danger as well as I did, but he barely acknowledged the newcomers' approach. Instead, he dropped his sword to the ground and grabbed my head in both of his hands. "Mai, you *owe* me," he growled.

And my debt slapped me in the face like a bucket of ice water. My voice—jerked free of the Master's grip for one split second—spouted powerful words.

"I, Mai Fairchild, swear to protect and uphold the Atwood pack to the best of my ability...."

Then the hold on my spirit that had been shaken by Gunner's debt was shattered. Blood flooded my mouth as I bit down as hard as possible on the inside of the male I possessed's cheek.

And as power rushed through me, wolves streamed past me. Gunner grunted as he fell beneath their assault.

"No!" I yelled...or thought...or murmured.

Then I slipped out of the body I'd been inhabiting and floated away into the void.

Chapter 40

When Liam pushed me out of my skin previously, I'd hovered disembodied for only a split second. This time, however, the darkness surrounded me for so long I thought I'd misgauged the ability of shared blood to pull me to my sister's side.

At least I wasn't back in my own body to be pushed around by the Master. At least I wasn't on that battlefield being forced to fight a werewolf I wanted instead to help.

Still, it was agonizing to wait there in nothingness. But then words flowed out of the darkness, proving that Kira—and I by proxy—was merely sitting quietly in the forest without a light.

"Don't you think it would be more fun to hang out by the campfire?"

"Not really," I felt and heard myself—my sister—answer the social worker. "Bigfoot isn't going to come near a campfire. Surely even you know that?"

As Kira spoke, she raised one hand to scratch her nose...and the effort, I sensed, was nearly enough to topple our shared body to the earth. Wherever we were, however we'd gotten here, my sister was *not* the chirpy, carefree teenager I'd left behind.

No wonder I felt so at home in her body. Because my spirit felt as weak as my sister's when I imagined Gunner falling on that hilltop beneath a wave of bloodthirsty wolves.

Stephanie, of course, was oblivious to all subtext. So she had nothing to react to other than the snarkiness in my sister's voice. "Kira," the social worker admonished.

And even though the pending adoption seemed like a vague storm cloud on a distant horizon at the present moment, loyal pack mates quickly jumped in to smooth down my sister's rough edges. "What she means..." Crow started, before petering out as he failed to think of a way to make Kira's insubordination palatable.

Luckily, Allen was ready to fill in gaps with a profusion of information that effectively muddied the trail. "...is that cryptozoology is a common hobby. Bigfoot, the Loch Ness monster, and more minor species such as the adjule and bunyip are fun to research and hunt for even though we know they don't exist in the wild. It's no different from practicing stage magic. Knowing what's real and what's myth doesn't make the latter any less entertaining as a hobby to cultivate."

"Simon *did* say something strange was going on in your family...." Stephanie's cagy tone suggested she was reacting to more than Kira's ill-badly chosen comment. Or perhaps the social worker was merely taken aback by Allen's dissertation on cryptozoology. Either way, it was enough to take my thoughts away from Gunner for a few brief seconds. And to make me wish I could see the human woman's face.

Just like that, my fingers—Kira's fingers—flicked the switch on the flashlight that had been sitting in our lap. The glow was painfully bright after so long in darkness, but not so blinding that I couldn't see a flash of motion off to our right....

Elle. Of course. How had I forgotten who else would be present on this supposed camping trip? How could I have not wondered whether the Master's sister was in league with her twin's plans?

Only Elle gave me no reason—beyond her genetics—for me to doubt her motives. Instead, she bent her neck toward me, averted her eyes in submission. Then, filling her voice with hidden meaning, she said, "I think I need to pee. Kira, care to tag along?"

I WASN'T QUITE SURE what I'd done to give away my presence, but Elle definitely knew who was hiding behind my sister's eyeballs. Kira, on the other hand, just as definitely did not.

Because the child went with the flow until she and Elle were far enough from the others so human ears couldn't overhear our conversation. Then she dropped the flashlight she'd used to guide us, her hand shaking as if touching the plastic had stung.

"I didn't turn on that light!"

My sister's panic surged through me, her body quivering just like her voice had done. She was weak as a newborn kitten. Perhaps because the Master was draining Mama's star ball back at the gathering, turning Kira wan and pale by proxy?

"I know," Elle started, less interested in Kira's physical weakness than in her emotional distress. "I think...."

But Kira was past the point of listening to reason. "Then get it out of me!" she demanded, slapping her cheeks so hard the sting brought tears to our eyes.

And, for one instant, I returned to the hilltop. I could almost hear the growling and tearing as the carnage I'd already witnessed flashed before of my eyes.

Or...maybe I really could hear the battle. Was that why my sister had been sitting in the darkness away from any campsite? Had she talked the guys into creeping as close as they could safely come to the meeting hill?

If so, there was a sliver of a chance that these few shifters could turn the tide in Gunner's favor. But only if I could get my sister to stop batting at her face and let me speak with her tongue.

"Out, out, out!" my sister was wailing. And I hoped that Stephanie's hearing was worse than that of the average middle-aged human. Otherwise, we'd have a lot of explaining to do once we returned from this supposed bathroom break.

Elle must have had the same thought. Because she grabbed our slender wrists with firm fingers. Held our hands away from our eyes. "You know it's your sister inside you, Kira."

"I don't!" the child started, speaking in gasps and bursts of emotion. "It could be anybody! It could be the *bad guy*!"

And even though I didn't want to scare my sister further, I seized her vocal cords and spoke through both of us. "Don't be a doofus, bedhead. This is really me."

For a moment, the forest fell silent around us. Then, our shared voice asked plaintively, "Mai?"

There was no time to soothe her, so I spit out facts short and not-so-sweetly. "Gunner is in trouble. Liam is the Master.

He controls half of the shifters at the meeting hill. They're trying to mow the others down at this moment...."

"Then we'd better help Gunner." Kira was as resilient and decisive as ever, never mind the fact that her knees wobbled as she stooped to grab the flashlight off the ground. I wanted to tell her that *she* wasn't going anywhere, that *she* was going back to camp and crawling into a sleeping bag until everything was over.

But the abrupt increase in illumination brightened our surroundings enough so we could see what the preceding drama had made us all miss. Stephanie had apparently decided to join the girls' pee party. And now she stared wide-eyed at Kira, who to all appearances was carrying on a conversation with herself.

"Simon was right. You *are* so much more troubled than any of us thought possible...."

"No," Elle started. "You don't understand."

Then, to my horror, Kira dove toward the other shifter and bit down hard on my mentor's wrist.

Chapter 41

I tasted the faintest hint of blood, then I was reeling from a slap to my cheek that should rightfully have knocked me earthward. Only, someone was holding onto my shoulders. Or, not holding—that was the icy hug of possession as Mama spoke through my lips.

"Yes, Master," she and I said together. And I shivered as I realized all of my efforts to escape the battlefield had been for naught. I was back under the control of a crazy, power-hungry shifter, and this time Mama was the one making my body move.

In desperation, I tried to lock my knees but instead found myself pacing the Master step for step as we neared the sounds of werewolves fighting. Vaguely, I noted that Liam and I must have been walking for most of the time I'd been absent from my body. Because we were back at the edge of the gathering hill, all signs of ceremonial hunt long since eradicated.

Geography was the least of my concerns, however, since a rising moon now revealed a sea of furry bodies, lunging, biting, tearing...dying. I couldn't see a single two-legger, nor anyone who appeared to be in touch with their rational senses. Gunner was similarly invisible, either lost in the melee or lost entirely beneath an avalanche of teeth and claws.

And I knew, in that moment, that whoever was winning, the unity of the Atwood pack had already been irrevocably broken.

Only...perhaps I'd been too hasty in my assessment. Because even as I took in a full breath of Atwood-flavored ozone, the fury of battle eased. And, beside me, Liam swore as he fumbled in his pocket before removing a vial and popping a cork out of the bottle's neck with his teeth.

The rich scent of blood rose between us, the cork returning to Liam's pocket unneeded. Then my captor was tilting the vial over his head to decant the contents, the boost of power Mama had worked so hard to harvest inches from his lips.

I couldn't let Liam top up his magic and hasten the battle before him...but I couldn't stop him either. Because my body was frozen just as he'd left it, inattention insufficient to break through the spell.

On the other hand, the bottle was nearly empty. And old blood doesn't flow like water, the last drop instead oozing down the glass wall so slowly that Liam was forced to tap the bottom violently in an effort to knock it loose.

"Lazy harlot," he growled, blaming my mother for...what? For failing to possess additional pack princesses and use sexual favors to lull shifter males into parting with their life fluids?

The insult was rude...and powerful. Because a kitsune honors her debts, but she doesn't have to obey a disparaging master.

And Mama must have been waiting for exactly that moment. Because invisible, icy fingers brushed over my hand momentarily...then I was abruptly freed from external control.

For half a second, I hesitated, gauging my path forward. If I killed Liam now, would Elle ever forgive me? Surely there was a less-than-fatal way to bring this struggle to an end....

Then the drop worked its way out of the bottle and onto the tongue beneath it. And, beside me, Liam began to laugh.

Which is when I realized we were in the midst of the dreamscape I so strongly remembered. Blood, moonlight, forest...and the Master before me smiling as he morphed Mama's star ball into a whip.

THE LASH OF MAGIC BIT through my clothes and into the skin beneath it, burning and freezing at the exact same time. Liam wasn't wearing a cloak and I wasn't wearing a kimono. Still, I felt myself being dragged forward just like in the dream as he murmured, "Come."

Mama was no longer possessing me, so I didn't have to obey this order. Still, the whip was unyielding as I dug in my heels and tried to wriggle my arms free of the magical noose. My star ball turned into a wedge and slid between the loops of the binding...only to begin dissolving as my captor's whip drained energy from me through it.

Shocked, I sucked in my remaining magic just as Liam grabbed onto my wrist, putting me back in the same predicament I'd started in. "You'll regret it if you disobey me," my captor growled, physically pulling me through the battling shifters on his way up the hillside. He was moving so quickly that the wolves around us didn't look up from their opponents long enough to decide we were worth a second glance. Still...impinging upon my personal space was my captor's first mistake.

Because I'd learned fighting long before possessing a star ball. Even with my arms bound around me, I wasn't defenseless, nor was I weak.

I bided my time, though, until we achieved the hilltop, the ground bloody but the area strangely vacant since the majority of the battle had drifted off to the western side. And as we crested the peak, the Atwood wolves were momentarily occluded by the steepness of the slope between us. Instead, all that met my eyes was dark canopies barely illuminated by the crescent moon...exactly the view I remembered from my dream.

When all of this is over, I need to ask Elle about kitsune foresight, I thought randomly. And then, without even warning myself that an attack was coming...I struck.

One leg hooked itself around Liam's left calf muscle. Meanwhile, the heel of my other foot pounded into his knee. I had no way of keeping myself upright, but at least my opponent plummeted also....

We fell to the earth in a tangle, Liam grunting—a disappointment since I'd been going for a kneecap-shattered howl. For a moment, either one of us might have come out triumphant. But I only had my legs to work with while he had use of both free hands.

Sure enough, tight fingers settled around my neck less than half a minute later. The Master's breath hissed as he whispered in my ear.

"Don't think you're irreplaceable. I already own another kitsune," Liam warned me. "Now watch...and learn."

Then one of his hands drifted a little higher until its fingers pinched my chin and twisted my head ninety degrees sideways. For a moment, I thought this was just another werewolf domination ritual. But then I noted a wolf standing eerily still in the middle of the battlefield....

"An eye for an eye," the Master continued. Then, releasing my chin, he snapped his fingers...and the wolf we'd been watching flipped its head back into an entirely unnatural posture before crumpling to the earth.

Chapter 42

"Here's how we're going to play this," Liam continued, rising off me and not bothering to offer a hand as I lay prone at his feet. Instead, he dusted off his clothing, reminding me that he was the only werewolf present who hadn't needed to shift in order to make his mark.

"You're going to pierce your own finger and give me some blood to start with," he explained, cadence overly patient as if speaking to a child. "Then you're going to squeeze out enough to fill this vial for snack time later on."

Demand and insult imparted with equal facility, the glass container dropped out of his fingers and grazed my forehead. The pain was immediate, but I was more interested in analyzing the contents as the bottle rolled off into the grass.

It was empty, meaning that Liam's borrowed magic was fading. If I delayed just a little longer, would the werewolves below us regain their senses and stop tearing into their kin?

"Look at me when I speak to you." Liam's words were backed up by a squeeze of the magical noose that bound me, and I struggled onto my knees in an effort to prevent another cautionary tale.

Because the Master's magic was still effective at this moment—I could hear the results behind my back. How much heel-dragging would Liam accept before he provided another example of his power? Would Tank be the wolf he chose to murder next?

As if following my thought processes, Liam smiled widely, reaching toward me with a needle in his hand. I wanted to snipe at him verbally, to tell him he was an idiot for binding my arms then expecting me to reach forward with appendages that were currently glued on either side of my torso. But all I could think about was Tank's earnest efforts to talk the judge around to giving me custody of Kira. So I struggled against the magical coils, attempting to obey the Master's wordless command.

And the effort was apparently acceptable. Because Liam laughed a deep, throaty chortle that was pure amusement at my terror and chagrin. "Ah, yes. How silly of me," he murmured. And as easily as that, the magical cord around me loosened, slipping back to its master like a retreating snake.

I was free of the physical binding but Liam smiled and rubbed his thumb absently across his four fingers, as if itching for the opportunity to teach me another lesson by taking an innocent's life. So, rather than attacking, I rose slowly and accepted the needle with my right hand.

The sliver of metal beneath my skin was a mere pin prick, nothing compared to the agony I'd feel once Liam used my blood to amp up the battle below. As if to prove that point, a howl rose from behind me. Higher pitched than the others, more of a yipping yelp morphing into a scream....

Meanwhile, before me, Liam reminded me of my duty. "Now hold out your finger," he demanded, his voice smooth again now that I'd started obeying him.

Something about the recent howl made me want to turn and peer across the battlefield. But our current detente was precarious, and I didn't dare to make any obvious move. Instead, I tried to get Liam talking. "I don't understand why you need to use Ransom as a puppet," I prodded, hating the fact that my voice quavered. "Surely you're strong enough to rule this pack by yourself....?"

Unfortunately, my captor didn't feel the need to explain himself the way he had earlier. Instead, he merely crooked one finger and raised both brows.

I could think of no solution save obeying him. So, hating every instant, I lifted my arm and offered up the bubble of blood pooling atop my skin.

This was it. The moment my weakness finished breaking my pack mates....

But Liam didn't accept the offering. Instead, he winced and turned sideways. His hand rose to his face. And when he removed the protective fingers and peered at them, even I could see the dark coating of blood.

Blood? Who could possibly have injured Liam from such a distance?

It made no sense because the hilltop was empty save for me and Liam. And Mama—but she was back beneath the Master's thumb. So what....?

Almost afraid to take my eyes off the Master, I nonetheless turned to peer back at the battlefield. And as I did so, I understood at once what had turned the tide.

Because there was a two-legger standing at the edge of the forest. Stephanie—the human social worker—had her mouth wide open as if she was shrieking words not quite loudly enough to reach me over the din between us.

Meanwhile, leaping from wolf to wolf like a child on a trampoline, a red-furred fox was nipping animal after animal on the nose.

KIRA WASN'T MERELY nipping. She was also licking. And as she swiped her long, pink tongue across yet another bamboozled werewolf's nostrils, the veneer of culture Liam had formerly dragged atop his rotten core wafted entirely away.

"You little bitch," the Master growled. But while his words were heated, they weren't steady. Instead, each scratch and lick clearly weakened him. I could see the effects as easily as if Liam had a magical meter pasted to the center of his forehead.

He swayed, cringed, barely managing to remain erect. Still, he wasn't so far gone that he couldn't fight against the damage. Thrusting his hand forward, he cast an inaudible order over the crowd.

A neck didn't snap this time; teeth did. Werewolf teeth one millimeter away from Kira's toes. Previously, the fighting had been dispersed and erratic. But now, at least half the shifters beneath us converged upon my sister as she spun sideways, pushed off balance by the unexpectedly united front.

Vaguely, I noted that Stephanie was forcing her way among the wolves in search of Kira. A flash of movement to one side was likely Crow or Allen in lupine form doing a better job beating a path toward their shared goal.

But they didn't have time to reach her. Not when Liam could see across the field with no obstructions and still had dozens of werewolves obeying his beck and call.

He'd forgotten me though. Had forgotten that the blood welling up out of my finger hadn't yet bound us back together. Had forgotten that his nosebleed continued unabated and he was currently flinging life fluids hither and yon.

All it took was a twist of my head to capture the first particle. All it took was one droplet landing on my tongue to break me free entirely.

And this time I didn't worry about Elle's hurt feelings. I didn't consider the possibility of Liam stealing my magic and using it to worsen his current depredations.

Instead, I thought only of the pack splintering around us. Then, pulling my star ball into sword form, I swung toward my opponent's jugular and mowed the Master down.

Chapter 43

My sword hit spine and lodged there. But lack of forward momentum was irrelevant, because Liam was already dead.

And as he crumpled to the ground beside me, Mama's magic oozed out of his body right alongside spurting blood. At first, the spray of bodily fluids was so intense I didn't even know what was happening. But then, somehow, my mother gathered enough energy to speak.

"Mai. I'm going. I'm almost gone. Kira...."

I immediately understood what my mother was telling me, but I couldn't seem to breathe sufficiently to do anything about it. Because Mama was right—she was already fading around the edges. The glowing star ball at her center was dimming as her fingers wisped away into the night.

Clods of dirt raining down upon a closed coffin. My father's tall body beside my own. My newborn sister relentlessly crying....

Mama had willingly ceded her body thirteen years earlier for the sake of my sister. Despite my current pain, I couldn't be the one responsible for turning that sacrifice into Kira's untimely death.

So I tore my gaze away from my mother's spirit. Screamed my sister's name across the field...

...Or, rather, croaked it. Because my face was wet, I realized, tears streaming down my cheeks and throat choked up too tight to speak normally.

Forcing air into my lungs, I tried one more time. "*Kira*. I need you up here *immediately*."

The tone that emerged was the same one I used to halt homework procrastination. Luckily, this time it had a better than usual effect.

Because the battle below was ending. Without Liam to pull the strings, wolves were pausing, shaking their heads in bemusement, then beginning to shift to their more rational form. Meanwhile, Stephanie had taken advantage of the confusion to pick her way between former combatants, and Crow had already reached my sister's side.

The latter met my eyes with steady willingness. Then, without even glancing to his alpha for permission, he grabbed Kira's fox body up like a football and swung her with all his might toward the top of the hill.

Kira must have drunk pints of blood in the preceding moments in order to manage a shift after being drained so thoroughly. But the exhilarating power coursing through her didn't make her laugh and play the way she usually would have. Instead, her brows furrowed and her eyes widened as she plummeted toward me. My sister had matured in the hours we'd been apart.

She'd matured, but she still possessed the needle-sharp claws bound to tear into me when she landed. I braced myself for the scratches...only Kira didn't scratch me because she didn't reach me. Instead, she flew through what remained of

Mama's star ball, and the magic grabbed hold and refused to let loose.

Light embraced the fox that was my sister. For half a second, incorporeal fingers smoothed fur away from wide, dark eyeballs.

Then, Kira regained her humanity, a vibrant glow of health blushing cheeks that had been white and sickly just an hour earlier. And, just like that, Mama was entirely gone.

WE'D LOST AND WON ALL in the same moment. And all I wanted was to enfold my only surviving family member into my arms.

Kira, on the other hand, had other thoughts about the matter. "This is so cool!" she hooted, her earlier quietness erupting into joy as she opened her hand to reveal a star ball subtly different from the borrowed one that used to follow her around our apartment. That magical orb had stuck to Kira's heels but had never obeyed her transformation orders. This one, in contrast, molded in the blink of an eye into the form of a tremendous, curving blade.

"Woo hoo!" she started, then her hoot transitioned into a gurgling "Ergh!".

Because even though we were a sword-wielding family, neither of us had any idea what to do with a scimitar. So it was no surprise that the ax-like widening at the tip of the materialized magic overbalanced my sister. The newly created weapon swung downwards as she fumbled...and nearly lopped off a couple of my fingers as it dropped.

"Oopsie," Kira finished unapologetically before swiping the weapon sideways and adding serrations to the blade that caused a strangle whistling noise. But I'd already lost track of her enthusiasm, the prickling of hairs on the back of my neck proving that a magic-happy teenager was the least of my concern.

"Kira," I warned. And without another glance at her glowing weapon, I took a long step forward in front of her. My body, I hoped, would be enough to shield my sibling from danger...which came in the form of dozens of shifters now clambering up the side of the hill.

Most were two-legged, which should have been a relief after the animalistic battle that had recently ended. But there was something worse about knowing the rapidly approaching werewolves were in their right minds...and still intent upon a kill.

"*They* did this to us. Kitsunes."

Their leader wasn't an Atwood, but he *was* someone I recognized. Edward, the older male who had gathered forces from the village to assist Gunner's strike.

Which meant he was on our side...or should have been. But Edward's eyes focused on the glowing scimitar in Kira's hand for one split second before boring into my forehead. "Both of you are kitsunes," he decided, having apparently understood more of the preceding moments than I would have expected. "You turned brother against brother within our pack."

It was hard to tell through the grime and wounds of battle, but it appeared that several of Edward's compatriots had recently fought on the opposite side. Healing scratches marked Liam's lackeys—no wonder they were ready to tear into me and Kira to prevent similar possession from ever happening again.

"Kira, go," I ordered, my own star ball taking longer than I would have liked but eventually materializing into my tried and true weapon. It wasn't a flashy scimitar, but it would get the job done.

Only Kira didn't move...and no wonder with the scent of ozone popping up behind both of my shoulders. I didn't even have to look to know two brothers now flanked me—Gunner on the right side, Ransom on the left.

The only surprising part was who spoke first—the older sibling's voice loud enough to carry easily to the back of the approaching force. His words, however, were about what I expected. "See, little brother. *This* is why you are unsuited to rule."

Chapter 44

A week ago, pack had been something foisted upon me. Despite Gunner's best efforts, I'd flitted around the outside of his crew's unity, uncertain how I felt about them folding Kira closer and closer into their midst.

Now, though, I understood what it meant to literally stand between two brothers. The ties of blood and pack binding the duo together were palpable...and I could almost see that connection radiating out across all of the shifters currently joining us atop the hill.

Because every shifter who could walk or limp was climbing up behind Edward now. There were far too many crumpled bodies left lying, but no one stayed to assist allies or enemies they picked their way past. Instead, as one being, werewolves were drawn to the heart of the pack's power...and to the disagreement that had nearly succeeded at cracking that heart in twain.

Nearly, but not quite. Or so I hoped, based on the fact that Ransom was still needling his brother verbally rather than finishing the job he'd recently started. Both brothers were still standing, which meant the role of clan leader was still in doubt.

"Is that how you see it?" Gunner murmured before diving directly to the core of what his brother had insinuated. "You consider loyal kitsunes a weakness rather than a strength?"

"Loyal?" Ransom laughed shortly then peered across the crowd. "Who here thinks these vixens are *loyal* to anything other than their own best interests? Who here would sleep a wink knowing kitsunes lived in the house next door?"

For a moment, all shifters remained silent. Then Tank's voice spoke up from somewhere to the left of center. "I slept very well one floor below kitsunes," he asserted.

"As did I," Allen called from way down at the bottom of the hill.

In contrast, the angry murmurs closer up were daunting. And despite my best intentions to keep a low profile and try not to make matters worse for Gunner, I took a step backwards and grabbed my sister's arm.

Because when it came right down to it, I would do whatever it took to protect Kira. Gunner, I knew, would eventually understand.

I didn't immediately drag my sister to safety, however, planting my feet and waiting for Gunner's reaction instead. He'd sidestepped this issue so gracefully and often over the course of the spring and early summer that I fully expected him to repeat the maneuver now that it really mattered. He'd assist me and Kira in making our escape then glue the clan back together. After all, pack meant everything to an alpha werewolf.

Or so I thought until Gunner willingly broke families apart all around us.

"Then we have nothing in common after all," Gunner answered, his voice carrying easily to every listening shifter. "Those who feel as my brother does are free to follow him. Pack up your houses, your families, take anything that's yours by tomorrow lunchtime and go.

"But if you're smart," the younger Atwood brother continued, his voice sad but no quieter, "you'll think it over. Talk to your parents, your mate, your children and decide whether it's really so bad to live check-to-jowl with kitsunes."

He paused, the air around us seeming to suck into his body as every audience member held their breath, waiting. Then, finally, Gunner finished his thought.

"Because if you leave now, it's a forever decision. The Atwood clan will not welcome traitors back."

I HALF EXPECTED RANSOM to fight against his brother's edict. After all, the elder brother had wanted the full Atwood power, not whatever portion of it came with carving a new territory from outpack land.

But when I took my eyes off my sister long enough to look at Ransom head-on for the first time since the battle ended, I saw that the older brother literally had no leg to stand on. There was blood streaming down his temple and gashes all over his body. Meanwhile, Ransom's left calf bent at an unnatural angle, only the efforts of two other shifters holding him erect.

There would be no more fighting between the brothers. Not tonight. Not when Ransom couldn't walk without help.

But that didn't prevent the elder brother from following up on Gunner's ultimatum. "If you're *smart*," he told the crowd at large, "you'll leave now with me rather than bedding down with *foxes*."

Then, without a single glance at his younger brother, Ransom fell forward onto three legs. The fourth tucked up beneath him, and he hop-stepped forward through the crowd as regally as any alpha wolf.

So, yes, Ransom had the wounded-warrior thing going for him. But one day earlier, Gunner possessed the full loyalty of every other shifter in this territory. One day earlier, if the younger brother had stood up and declared himself pack leader, no one except his brother would have batted an eyelash before bowing to their new lord.

But now, hands drifted down to touch the vanquished brother's fur as he pressed past his pack mates. And far too many glanced once at me and Kira before turning to follow Ransom away from the life they'd cherished up until now.

The pain of the pack dissolving hit me like a blow to the solar plexus. But it was my little sister who made the demand I itched to dish out. "Gunner, *do* something. Mai and I can..."

Her voice petered out then, not just because there was no real solution but also because Gunner had taken the child into his arms and pressed his lips to her forehead. "It's not your fault," he murmured one inch from her skin, speaking almost too softly for me to hear him. "It's done. You're worth it. Now hush."

The gesture had been meant to comfort my sister, but it also consolidated the truth of Gunner's alliance with kitsunes. No wonder a sigh washed over the remaining shifters, the visible proof of their alpha's loyalties provoking yet more members of the audience to break away.

And still Gunner did nothing. Not even when a figure began moving toward us out of the dwindling gathering, materializing into Elle as she stopped directly in front of her half-brother's nose.

"I have to go with Ransom..." Gunner's cousin—half-sister—started. And for the first time I smelled a crack in the new pack leader's armor.

"Because I wasn't a brother to you." The alpha paused, swallowed. "I'm sorry for my part in your mother's loss."

"Don't be an idiot. It wasn't your fault." For half a second, Elle reached up to trail her hand across Gunner's cheek. Then she sighed and took one long step back. "But Ransom needs me more than you do...."

And Gunner was an alpha hardwired to protect his underlings. So he nodded, jerked his head into the half-darkness toward someone I couldn't make out in the distance. "Crow, go with your woman."

Then, just like that, half the werewolves I trusted were no longer part of our pack.

Chapter 45

"So this is what you were hiding."

Most of the nearby shifters had either followed Ransom or gone to tend to the injured by the time Stephanie made it to the top of the rise to join us. Which was probably a good thing, since the human had no concept of how to act around riled-up werewolves. Her flashlight slid across our faces, blinding me briefly and provoking the scent of fur from my companions. Then the beam settled resolutely at my sister's feet.

"Mrs. B..." Kira started. But the social worker talked right over the teenager, taking yet another step forward so she could wave a finger under Gunner's nose.

"Have you people never heard of pedophilia? Child endangerment? You really let a thirteen-year-old wander around with no clothes on where anyone can see?"

Clothes? After watching a pitched battle and shifters transforming from wolf to human, *this* was what Stephanie was most concerned about?

Luckily, Allen had us covered...quite literally. Unlike his pack mates, he hadn't shifted into animal form during the preceding battle. Which meant he was wearing human-appropriate clothing and possessed a backpack full of much-needed spare shirts.

"Big, bad wolf," read the one he tossed to Kira. Gunner shielded the child as she shrugged into the tent-like t-shirt, the large male's body seeming to shrink in on itself at the same time as he submitted in an entirely un-alpha-like manner to the social worker's wrath.

"I know what you saw today was upsetting," Gunner started....only to be silenced by Stephanie's "Eh, eh, eh."

"No, I don't want your explanations," the middle-aged matron rebutted. "The time for that would have been last week or last month. Around the time you invited me to that first cookout." Then, dismissing the alpha werewolf entirely, Stephanie pushed him aside so she could offer my sister much softer words. "The fact that you're a fox girl..."

"Kitsune," my sister countered quietly. Despite the clarifying interruption, her tone suggested even she was cowed by the official's disappointment and barely restrained rage.

"Kitsune," Stephanie repeated, sounding out the word slowly to make sure she said it correctly. "Whatever your heritage, child, you're my responsibility. And I think you should come with me right now...."

Abruptly, there were growling two-leggers all around us. Gunner, Tank, even Allen sounded like they were inches away from donning fur.

Which meant I was currently the sole rational party present. So, leaving Kira where she was, I stepped between the werewolves and Stephanie, trying to tell the social worker with my eyes that now was, perhaps, not the best time for making demands. "We can hash this out tomorrow," I offered. Because the idea of Stephanie spilling our secrets in human court was daunting...but it was better than watching her get ripped apart by my pack mates right now.

"You'll be there?" Stephanie's eyebrows rose while her mouth pursed pensively. I could see her point—fleeing might be wiser than continuing to fight for custody.

Yet, despite everything, I found myself nodding. "Yes. Please. Let Allen walk you to your car now and I *promise* that Kira and I will be there tomorrow in court." Immediately, this new oath tugged at my belly lighter but no less virulent than the one that used to tie me to the alpha behind my back.

And after one long moment, Stephanie bent her neck in regal approval. Human or not, she knew when to accept an oath as fact.

The social worker wasn't quite done with us, however. "You, Allen—you're a wolf also?" she asked over my shoulder. Then, without waiting for an answer, she shook her head and glared at the least offensive werewolf present. "It doesn't matter. I need a guide, so you will stay human until I'm safely in my car."

"Yes, ma'am," Allen promised, dropping the backpack but otherwise acting for all the world like a submissive werewolf obeying his alpha as he brushed past the rest of us. Then he was leading Kira's social worker toward the encircling forest...although not quickly enough to prevent her from tossing back one last jab at those she left behind.

"I will see you all in court," the decider of Kira's future promised. Then Stephanie was gone, a problem for another day.

"SO," GUNNER STARTED. And I didn't realize we were alone and naked until I heard Kira's receding giggle as she and Tank rooted through Allen's backpack in search of additional clothing.

"So," I answered, breathing in the alpha's enticing scent. There was more granite in his aroma than I was used to, his voice rough around the edges from the difficulties of the preceding hours.

But he was here and I was here. We'd both survived the battle...and there was one thing left undone.

"You need to pull your pack together," I told him. "Go back to clan central and talk to your people so they don't do anything stupid."

"Once you and Kira are settled," Gunner started. But I reached up and placed one finger atop his lips.

The skin there was soft but prickly around the edges where the barest beginning of a beard was starting to grow in. I wanted to lean in closer and see if his taste was as good as his aroma. But instead, I merely shook my head.

"Gunner, you're the pack leader. Kira and I can't be your top priority. A lot of your clan members don't have the first idea what to do around kitsunes. They'll leave with Ransom if we return with you right now."

"They'll stay if I tell them to," Gunner growled. But he didn't look into my eyes as he said it. He knew I was right.

"They might, but they'll resent it," I countered. "Wasn't that the whole point of letting Ransom take so many shifters with him just now?"

My voice wanted to break, but I instead took a deep breath and treated this like any other adulting situation. If I could force Kira to brush her teeth when she was sleep deprived, then I could make an alpha werewolf do his job.

"Kira and I will make ourselves scarce for a while," I started. "And then…."

"And then we'll cross that bridge when we come to it," I finished before Gunner started making promises he couldn't keep.

Because this was goodbye. Somewhere deep in my heart I knew it. So, without worrying about repercussions, I ensured there would be nothing for me to regret later. Grabbing onto Gunner's shoulders to steady myself, I eased onto tiptoes then I kissed those enticing lips.

Chapter 46

This kiss wasn't a distraction to keep Gunner from noticing my magic. Nor was it a claiming on his part. Instead, it was a sharing, an acknowledgement that we were more than mere pack mates.

And, in response, an explosion of stars flared behind my eyelids. The air filled with so much electricity I almost expected a lightning strike. This, right here, was as natural as breathing. I couldn't imagine why I'd fled from it for so long.

Then Gunner was pushing away from me, calling Tank toward him. "Take them back to the city. Protect them. Don't let either Mai or Kira out of your sight."

"Yes, pack leader." Tank's tone was so respectful he might as well have prostrated himself atop the bloody grass between us. And any thought I'd had of arguing that Gunner needed his faithful second as backup faded in the face of an alpha laying down the law.

Then we three were tramping back through the trees the way Kira and I had come two days earlier. It turned out that an easily traversable path paralleled our earlier bushwhacking, which—combined with Kira's newfound vigor—meant the journey went by far too fast.

Fast but not easy. Because every step yanked at my belly. Every step increased the spear of agony throbbing beneath my forehead. *I shouldn't be leaving my pack mates. I shouldn't be leaving Gunner.* So this is what it felt like to tie myself to were-wolves...then to let those same wolves go.

Sure enough, the pain worsened as we drove back toward the city, miles separating me from the place where the majority of my pack now resided. Gunner's mansion, when we reached it, was musty even though we'd been gone for less than seventy-two hours. And while the sun had long since risen and begun fading into afternoon, the residence struck me as painfully dark.

"The death count was minimal," Tank offered half an hour later as he came up behind me in the third-floor hallway. I was standing outside the closed door of the bathroom, listening to Kira brush her teeth and twitching every time the teenager went quiet for more than a second at a time. Because as much as it had hurt to leave Gunner, letting Kira out of my sight stung even worse....

"Minimal doesn't mean zero," I answered without bothering to turn and greet my minder. I knew Tank was trying to cheer me. But his words instead triggered a replay of Liam's object lesson, the one I'd been incapable of halting in time.

Snapping fingers, snapping neck. Me allowing wolves to tear into each other to prevent another from being unceremoniously murdered....

I shivered, pushing the memory into some dark corner of my mind to be chewed over later. Only then did I finish my thought. "And what percentage of the pack left with Ransom? What will happen to the clan now that it's been split in half?"

Tank didn't answer verbally. Instead, his fingers touched the nape of my neck momentarily, the fleeting contact a werewolf show of support.

Then Kira was pushing out of the bathroom in pajama bottoms and that same *Big, bad wolf* t-shirt she'd been wearing for hours. "Nap with me," she demanded, seemingly untouched both by the recent past and by the fact that her custody hearing began in just a few short hours.

And how could I deny her? Nodding once at Tank, I followed my sibling down the hall to her not-so-tastefully decorated bedroom. Fell into the princess-canopied bed and pulled the curtains around us before morphing into a fox.

Kira was already vulpine. Red fox tail covered her nose as she fell asleep instantly. And I curled around her slightly smaller body, completing our fluffy lump.

I didn't sleep though. Just lay there staring at the stick-on stars on the ceiling and wondering whether Kira and I were better off now than we had been three months earlier. To find a pack then lose it—was that really better than never having belonged at all?

Only Kira and I weren't really alone, even here in the echoing mansion. Because, two hours later, Tank tapped on the closed door between us. "Wake up, ladies," his deep voice urged us.

It was time to go to court.

"AND YOU ARE HAPPY WITH this document, Ms. Fairchild?" The judge speared me with a gaze so piercing that it knocked my attention—for one split second—off the social workers whispering adamantly to each other two rows back.

"Yes, Your Honor," I agreed. "I think 'godbrother' is a perfect representation of Gunner Atwood's relationship to my sister, now and in the future. I'm very grateful for his offer and willingly accept."

My voice only quavered slightly as I made the statement Tank had drilled into me during the short drive over, and not from a fox's urge for self-determination either. Instead, my separation from said godbrother was still gnawing at my stomach, making it hard to keep a pleasant smile pasted on my lips.

Meanwhile, I caught a single word drifting forward from Simon that further chilled my body. "*Werewolf*," my former social worker hissed adamantly, the mumble before and after that scathing indictment impossible to decipher. Stephanie's response, unfortunately, was drowned beneath the judge's subsequent statement, which boomed out fill the entire chamber with his voice.

"If I could have your attention," he ordered, sounding for all the world like an alpha-leaning werewolf. There was no zing to the command, though. No electricity that ran up my spine like spiders. Still, I resolutely closed my ears to the discussion behind me and apologetically bowed my head.

"Well," the decider of Kira's fate continued more cordially after flipping through the pages before him the way he'd already done three times previously. "Gunner Atwood's addition to this guardianship hearing *does* relieve some of my concerns about Kira's future. *But...*"

He paused theatrically, and it was Kira who pinched me when I raised my head and narrowed my eyes into a glare.

Right. Not getting into a fight with a human official...although if the judge ruled against us, all bets were off.

"...I understand the State has some reservations," the judge finished right about the time I'd decided strangling him wouldn't be so inappropriate. "Mrs. Baumgartner, would you like to speak next?"

"...of the *child.*" Simon apparently didn't know how to whisper, because the tail end of his final admonition was clear to all of us. The social worker's harrumph after the judge silenced him with raised eyebrows was similarly audible, but by that point Stephanie had come forward to the witness stand.

"Yes, Your Honor," Stephanie said, glancing at Kira out of the corner of one eye before squaring her shoulders and facing the judge directly. I could smell the human's dilemma, could tell that she was still wavering from the slump of her spine and the cock of her head.

In my experience, time tended to make the shock of the supernatural less biting. Unfortunately, the robed male on the bench didn't give Stephanie so much as a minute to make up her mind about the matter at hand.

"Well, put us all out of our misery," the judge demanded. "What is your official standpoint on the adoption of Kira Fairchild?"

Chapter 47

"I think that Kira Fairchild is a strong-willed young woman with great potential, and I'm honored to have spent even a few months as part of her life," Stephanie said after one additional, harrowing pause. Kira grabbed my right hand while Tank grabbed my left hand, and I wasn't sure whether they were offering support or holding me down.

Then the social worker's scent cleared and she glanced back again, this time with a smile on her lips as she met my eyes and then my sister's. "But my advice is to remove her from my caseload," Stephanie finished. "Kira's best with her own family, and she deserves to have those relationships she's created legally affirmed."

Then it was all over except the pictures. Well, that plus the paperwork, which Tank told me would be ready the following week.

In the meantime, my pack of three filtered out to the steps of the courthouse, jostling and smiling as the sun beat down upon our faces. "I knew we'd get custody as soon as Allen gave me the t-shirt," Kira proclaimed blithely, twisting her body as if modeling the pink sequined monstrosity that covered her torso and back. *"Favorite pup,"* the rear stated. And, much smaller, where a front pocket would have been located, words that I was glad the judge hadn't noted from the bench....

"Well, Boss Bitch, where do you want your glamor shoot?" Tank asked, pulling out his ubiquitous cell phone and flipping it into photo mode.

"Over here!" my neck-risking sister answered, leaping onto a balustrade at the edge of the grand porch we'd gathered in, not appearing to notice that she now hovered above a thirty-foot drop to hard stone ground. And while a human guardian would have grabbed Kira's foot to steady her, I was just glad to see the pack-separated sadness wiped away by her short nap.

Plus, Stephanie was walking out the front door now. So I merely mouthed *Be good* at my sister before hurrying over to thank the social worker before she could rush out of our lives.

"I really appreciate..." I started.

But the middle-aged woman interrupted me. "It's my job to make sure foster kids end up in the best placement for the sake of the child. Kira may be surrounded by wolves and blood and scary things I'm probably not aware of. But anyone can see she thrives as part of a pack."

Then the same human who had recently taken in the horror of a pack battle slipped out of her suit jacket, revealing unexpected words on the underlying blouse. *"Honorary Werewolf,"* the shirt stated. And for a moment my throat clenched up as I realized Allen been come prepared for all eventualities...except the one where he wasn't actually present with us now.

Winning the adoption battle without the rest of our pack beside us hurt so much I had to close my eyes for one split second. And by the time I'd widened my lips back into a smile, Kira's gaze had settled upon the human who made this entire photo shoot possible.

"Mrs. B!" my sister exclaimed. She'd been spinning in a circle atop the railing, hands out to either side like a tightrope walker. But now, she motioned Stephanie over. "Come be in the picture!" And, like a magnet, the teenager's enthusiasm drew both me and the social worker back to the marble ground beneath our charge's feet.

"Say cheese," Tank told us from five feet distant. And I really would have...if the front door of the courthouse hadn't opened at that exact same moment, sending the furry scent of stalking werewolf wafting over us all like summer heat.

I DIDN'T TURN MY STAR ball into a sword, though. Nor did I yank Kira off the ledge and push her toward Tank to hustle out of harm's way. Instead, my fake smile morphed into a cheek-splitting grin as just the werewolves I'd been thinking off stepped out into the light.

Gunner and Allen wore lettered t-shirts just like Kira's, but I didn't bother trying to read the words this time around. Instead, I only had eyes for the pack leader as he snagged a random bystander with a panty-melting smile and roped her into taking over Tank's spot as photographer of the hour.

Then the werewolf I'd missed the most was there beside me, his arm settling over my shoulder and pulling me in even closer as we all smiled for the camera's sake. "Sorry I was late," he murmured, his breath tickling my earlobe.

"I'm just glad you're here now." Then, remembering the reason I'd left him in the first place. "But your pack needs you...."

"Yes you do. And here I am."

I punched his arm before blinking at my own physical show of affection. What...was I turning into a werewolf now?

And, as if he'd been privy to my internal monologue, Gunner's smile went from blinding to supernova, so warm it beat against my skin.

"Everyone who hasn't left with my brother will still be there tomorrow," he said, answering my real concern, albeit belatedly. "But Kira's adoption only happens once. I figured it was about time I learned to act like a fox and wiggle around the rules when necessary. Everyone who loves your sister should be here for her special day."

And everyone was...almost.

Because the spot where Crow and Elle should have stood remained empty. Meanwhile, the stress from leaving the Atwood pack unattended at such a critical moment was visible in Gunner's creased brow.

But all I saw when I looked at that photo days and weeks and years later was Kira's joyous kitsune nature as she leapt off the railing without warning and was caught quite easily by five pairs of waiting hands. All I heard in my memory was Gunner's voice whispering into my ear.

"A pack is only as weak as its strongest member."

I could only hope he was right.

From the Author

Did you enjoy *Shadow Wolf*? If so, I hope you'll consider taking a moment to leave a review while you wait for this trilogy's final installment to launch in January 2019.

Meanwhile, if you missed it, there are three other series set in this same werewolf world: the Wolf Rampant Trilogy, the Alpha Underground Trilogy, and the Wolf Legacy Quartet. Of these, the first book in the Wolf Rampant series, *Shiftless*, is a great place to start since it's free on all retailers in ebook format.

You can also download a free starter library and explore unique extras when you sign up for my email list at www.aimeeeasterling.com.

Thanks for reading! You are why I write.

Printed in Great Britain
by Amazon